WHATEVER HAPPENS

MICALEA SMELTZER

To the real "Mr. Rochester"

Thank you for being a teacher I admire and look up to. You encouraged me to follow my dreams when others thought I was crazy. I'll never ever forget that.

CHAPTER ONE

Stepping out of the massive SUV, my worn purple Vans touch down on the crumbling asphalt outside my new home.

The new house, unlike the road in front, isn't falling apart.

It's a pristine, newly renovated, modern looking farmhouse.

It looks too sparkly and lifeless to me. It's beautiful, sure, but it's not my home.

My home is miles and miles away in the rearview mirror.

My parents wanted to escape the memories. I wanted to drown in them.

Now, we'd moved all the way from Texas to a small town not far from Cambridge, Massachusetts. The bank my dad worked for as the head of IT paid for the move, and the massive moving truck rolled to a stop behind the Escalade.

"What do you think?" The passenger door closes softly and my mom steps up beside me, sizing up the house. Her voice is soft, not filled with any sort of joy at all, mostly just a tone of resignation.

"It's a house," I answer resolutely, exhaling a small sigh.

A house is four walls encapsulating emptiness. A home is the people, the laughter, the memories. This home doesn't have any of that. It's merely a shell.

"It's a house," she echoes.

My dad joins us at my other side. None of us speak to the notable absence between us.

It's been three months, nearly four, since my little sister took her own life. The tragedy still dangles over the three of us like the guillotine I learned about in my history and French classes.

We barely speak of her nonexistence, all grieving in our own ways and unable to talk about it. I've tried, but my dad shuts down and my mom bursts into tears at the mention of Luna.

"Should we check it out?" Dad cocks his head to the side, his hands on his hips. His dark blue pants and white button down are loose on his normally broad frame. He's lost weight since my sister died. "What do you say, Vi?" He forces a smile, but it's not like the wide one he used to sport.

"Lead the way." I plaster on a smile as well.

All of us are puppets right now. We don't know how to function without Luna. She was the light, life, the stars itself. She shined brighter than anyone I knew.

Before following my parents up the driveway, I open the car door and grab the small travel cage holding my beloved pet ferret. I get him out, cradling him in my arms.

"Well, Will Ferret, welcome to our new home."

He looks back at me with his small black eyes and I swear he even cocks his head to the side like he knows what I'm saying.

"Vi, hurry up." Dad waves from the steps of the front porch and I hurry to catch up.

When I join them he swings the front door open, revealing a foyer with vaulted ceilings, an L-shaped staircase, and dark wood floors spanning from the foyer to the rest of the house.

Tilting my head back, I take in the chandelier above. It's black, wrought iron maybe, and reminds me of something you might see in a Spanish style home.

I follow my parents from room to room as they point out each and every one, talking about where they plan to put pieces of furniture from our old house.

It's all so normal, but not.

We wouldn't even be here if Luna was still alive.

Will wiggles in my arms and I let him down. He thinks he's a dog and runs around the house most of the time when I'm home anyway.

Dad steps up to the row of windows overlooking the backyard and a field beyond. His hands are on his hips and he lets out a heavy breath. My heart clenches, because I know he's thinking of Luna. We all always are.

I stop beside him, and he tilts his chin down to me before wrapping an arm around my shoulders. "What do you think, kiddo? Think you'll like it here?"

I miss home, this place is a stranger to me, but suddenly I understand why my parents were so adamant about this. Maybe it's exactly what we all need. A fresh start.

I smile at him. "I think it'll be perfect, Dad."

He wraps me in a hug and I bury my face against his chest, inhaling the scent of our laundry detergent.

I never want to let go, because I'm afraid if I do my feet might never touch the earth again.

CHAPTER TWO

Hours later all the furniture is in the house and boxes are strewn about.

Sitting at the top of the stairs I can hear my parents arguing in the kitchen about some vase my mom is freaking out didn't get packed, while my dad insists he personally packed it himself and it's just been mislabeled or placed in the wrong room.

My parents have never fought often, and they were always open with Luna and I when they did. They wanted us to know marriage isn't easy and you're not always going to agree, but you do have to love each other enough to get through it.

I hope they can love each other enough to get through this. I lost a sister, but they lost a child. Come next year, I'll be gone too. College looms over me like a heavy cloud. I used to be excited to start that chapter of my life, but not anymore. It seems so trivial when living is so important.

Standing up, I turn around and head down the hall to my room. The walls are white, but I don't mind. Soon enough they'll be covered in posters and photos.

My bed sits against the back wall and the window to the left overlooks the backyard and has a portion of roof I can open the window and climb out on to sit. I'm thankful for that. My room back home had it, and I always liked sitting out there looking at the stars. When my emotions get too big I like to look at the stars, the universe, and be reminded of how small we really are.

Will Ferret's large playhouse sits on the floor for the time being.

My dresser is across from the bed with a mirror above and my desk is tucked into the corner. The table Will Ferret's cage goes on is stationed between the doors to my closet and bathroom.

A gray fluffy rug is rolled up in the corner of the room with ample boxes scattered around.

"Well, Will, I better get started on this." *Or else I'll be sleeping on a bare mattress.*

I grab the box cutter I brought up with me an hour ago when I intended to start unpacking my room, but things got overwhelming and I had to take a breather.

Starting with the box labeled BEDDING I unpack my sheets and quilt. Another box contains my pillows. Once I have everything I need, I make my bed and already the room looks more like an actual bedroom.

Will watches me from the floor and I wish I could lift

his cage myself up onto the table, but it's large and awkward, which means I'll need my dad's help.

After my bed's made and looks halfway decent I start on the boxes containing my clothes. It takes a good two hours to get all of my clothes put into the closet and stuffed in my dresser.

I slide one of the dresser drawers closed and as it clatters into place my mom calls out my name. "Violet! Pizza is here!"

I didn't even know they'd ordered pizza, but my stomach comes to life, growling like a little gremlin lives there.

"Be good, Will." His black little eyes follow me as I leave the room.

My feet pound down the steps and I ignore the fact there isn't an echoing of them behind me.

In the bright modern kitchen—white cabinets and white granite—I find two boxes of pizza on the bar top. Three barstools are already fixed in front.

Three, not four. My heart seizes in my chest and tears prick the back of my eyes. I cried every day after she died. Everything reminded me of Luna. Now, I'm better, but the strangest things will cause the pain to come flooding back.

I force myself to look away and realize they've almost completely unpacked the kitchen items. There are only two boxes left, with what looks like a million already taken down and stacked in the corner for recycling.

"Pizza, Vi." My mom breezes by me, shaking me from my thoughts. "Aren't you hungry?"

"Y-Yeah." My hands shake as I tuck a piece of long

brown hair behind my ear. Grabbing a plate stacked on the counter, I swipe two slices of pepperoni pizza and join my parents at the kitchen table to the right. It's surrounded by two walls of windows overlooking the backyard and the neighbor's house.

"Getting anything done?" Mom asks me, sprinkling red pepper flakes onto her pizza. Her hair is the same shade as mine. We actually look a lot alike. I have her pouty mouth and small nose, but my eyes are all my dad from their shape to icy blue color. With my dad's dark hair and olive skin his eyes really pop. I, however, inherited my mom's pale skin.

"Yeah, my clothes are unpacked and I made my bed. It's basically just books and odds and ends left."

"That's good." Her eyes crinkle at the corners with a smile. I nod along, not knowing what to say. Thankfully, for me, she carries on the conversation. "Do you think you'll try out for the cheer team here?"

I've been a cheerleader since seventh grade and before that I was in gymnastics from the time I was three. I always loved tumbling and flipping.

"No." The one word leaves me in adamant refusal.

Her eyes widen in surprise. "No? Why? This is your senior year. Surely, you want to do it your final year of high school. It seems a shame to give it all up."

"I don't want to," I bite out, my words cutting.

Her brows furrow and she opens her mouth to argue, but my dad clears his throat.

"I think it's fine you don't want to do it this year. Focus on your grades and college." He gives my mom a significant look to drop it and when his eyes connect with mine I know he understands there's more to it than me not wanting to do it.

"School starts in three weeks, what do you think you'll do between now and then?"

I pick apart the crust of my first slice of pizza. "I don't know. Explore the town. Maybe get a job."

"A job?" Her eyebrows raise.

"Yeah, I can save for a car."

"Honey, we told you we'd get you a car for graduation."

"I think if you want a job, that's a great idea. As long as it doesn't interfere with school."

I flash my dad a grateful smile for once again saving me. "It's just an idea. I might not have time. Maybe I'll join a club at school or something."

A wrinkle forms in Mom's forehead. "A job? Club? But not cheerleading like you've done for years. I don't under—"

"The pizza was great." I stand up with my plate. "I'm going to try to finish unpacking my room before I go to bed."

"Violet—"

I hear my dad whisper something to her as I dump the remains of my dinner in a trash bag lying on the floor, full of miscellaneous crap from the move.

Escaping upstairs I close the door to my room. It's seven in the evening but since it's summer, the sun hasn't even set yet.

Sitting down, I start on another box. I go through the photos in it, sighing as I look at pictures of me with girls I called my friends for years. Friends who I haven't heard from all summer. It's not like I couldn't have reached out, but it sucks when people don't know how to deal with your loss. I needed my friends to be there for me, to get me out of the house and remind me life goes on, but they didn't. People are terrified of saying or doing the wrong thing when you're grieving, when all you really want is to just have someone be there for you.

I debate on throwing the photos away, but decide against it and toss the photos in a desk drawer, piling more items on top.

I do stick other Polaroid's and photos on my walls. Photos of my parents, Luna, vacation beach trips, and even a funny one of Will and I when I was holding him in the air and he sneezed on me. My face is priceless. I touch the tips of my fingers to one of my favorite pictures. It's Luna and I when we're little, dressed in Disney Princess costumes—I'm Ariel and she's Aurora—and our faces are lit with happiness. The photo was taken at the exact moment my parents told us we were going to Disney World. Luna's small fists are clasped under her chin, her eyes alight with happiness, and the binky that was in her mouth is forever suspended in mid-air.

Tears burn my eyes and I dam them back.

I'm not sure I can ever forgive myself for not seeing the pain and sadness in my sister's eyes in those final months leading up to her suicide. Luna and I were always close, but that year we'd drifted apart. We still spoke and hung out some, but not like we used to. I was too focused on my friends, boys, parties, and cheer.

Now she's gone and I can't rewind time to make it right.

I close my eyes, remembering her last text message to me.

It's not your fault.

I'd been confused when I received the text message, wondering what wasn't my fault.

I got my answer when I arrived home an hour later to an ambulance, my mom wailing as my dad held her, and a body bag being wheeled out of the house.

CHAPTER THREE

Sleep evades me as I toss and turn in my bed, thinking if I find just the right spot sleep will magically take me.

Picking up my phone the time flashes back at me.

It's barely three in the morning and I've slept maybe five minutes.

I shove the blankets off and tiptoe over to the window. The windows are brand new and don't make a sound as I unlock and raise one so I can step out onto the roof.

I sit down, drawing my knees up to my chest and wrapping my arms around them.

Tilting my head back I take in the night sky above.

Stars wink back at me and I look until I find the brightest one in the heavens.

Luna, I think to myself. Ever since she passed I make a point to find the brightest star every chance I can, because she shined more than anyone I know and it makes me feel closer to her.

"I failed you, Moon." It was my nickname for my little sister.

I failed her, but I also failed myself. I became obsessed with popularity and being with the in crowd. So much so that I forgot what's really important.

I'll never make that mistake again.

I hear a noise and look down, searching.

I spot movement on the neighbor's patio and look down to see a dark head bent over a large telescope, one that looks like something a professional would use.

I watch the person, curious what it is that draws them to the stars like me.

As if sensing me, the person looks up and my lips part as the boy finds me. Floppy brown hair tumbles over his forehead and black-rimmed glasses slip down his nose. When his eyes find mine in the dark they quickly dart away.

He looks to be my age, but since it's dark I can't be quite sure.

He focuses on the telescope, but his shoulders are tight now, not relaxed like before. After a moment, he shakes his head, and without looking my way again he heads into his house.

With one last look at the sky, I decide I should do the same. I slip inside, closing and locking the window.

When I turn, I look out the window beside my bed and a light blinks on in the house next door as the boy enters his room.

Even though my room is dark, it's like he can sense me as he looks through the window. His gaze drops and he reaches for the blinds, rolling them down.

My mouth downturns, wondering what his problem is, but I have other things to worry about than my new unnamed neighbor.

Knowing I won't be getting any sleep tonight, I sneak from my room and get a head start on more unpacking.

At least it's something my parents won't have to do come morning.

———

"You did all this?"

I jolt upright from the spot I passed out, on the floor of the family room.

"Y-Yeah," I stutter, rubbing sleep from my eyes. The sun has completely risen and I smell coffee coming from the kitchen. My mom stands at the entrance to the room with her robe wrapped around her slender body. Her eyes shift around the room, taking in the décor items added to the built in shelves, her beloved fake plants I tell her only gathers dust, among other odds and ends. This isn't the only room that saw my touch during the early hours. I'm surprisingly productive when I'm running on adrenaline.

"Did you sleep?" Her eyes narrow on me and I know she doesn't need me to answer. "You need to rest, Vi."

"I'm fine, Mom." I stand up from the floor, placing my palms on the couch to give me leverage. "Can I have some of that coffee?"

She tosses her arm over her shoulder. "Go to bed."

"It's morning," I argue.

She pinches the bridge of her nose. "You have to sleep."

Tell me something I don't know.

"I'll sleep when I'm dead."

She flinches and my mouth parts in horror, realizing what I've said. In my tiredness my ill-placed joke slipped out of my mouth.

"Mom, I didn't mean—"

She holds up a hand, her silent command for me to shut up. She walks away without a word and I know I've hurt her. It was unintentional but that doesn't fix the mistake.

Wringing my worn pajama shirt in my hands I bite my lip in an effort to hold back tears. I can't do anything right anymore.

As quietly as I can, I slip upstairs to my bedroom and then the attached bath. I get into the shower, not even marveling over the shiny pearlescent looking tiles. When I finish I blow-dry my hair hastily, braiding it sloppily down my right shoulder. Dressing in a simple pair of jean shorts and a striped tank top I grab my purse, sliding it across my body before slipping my feet into a pair of flip-flops.

"Where are you going?" My dad questions as I pass him in the hall on the way to the stairs.

"Thought I'd go explore."

He tilts his head. "I thought I could make my world famous French toast for breakfast. I have a few days before I start work. I wanted to make the most of it."

"Thanks, Dad. I'll have some when I get back."

His face falls and he reaches for my arm when I start to walk away. I pause, my eyes reluctantly meeting his.

"I love you, you know that, right?"

"Of course, Dad. I love you, too."

His lips are downturned and his light hold on my arm doesn't lessen. A war rages in his eyes and finally he murmurs, "I'm sorry."

I flinch and he lets me go, hastily turning away but not before I see the pain on his face.

The pain we all keep hiding, pushing down into the deepest pits of our souls, until one day it's bound to turn into a black hole and swallow all of us alive.

I reach the bottom of the stairs and feel like I'm suffocating.

"I'll be back in an hour," I yell out, and don't wait for a response as I make a break for the garage. Inside I find my yellow bike with wicker basket tucked beside the wall amid boxes. I fish it out and one of the boxes falls. I hear a crash, but I don't stop to see what's broken.

Pressing the button on the garage door I make my escape.

I wanted to leave anyway, but now I *have* to.

Hopping on my bike I pedal as fast as I can away from the house and neighborhood of cookie cutter perfect homes.

It doesn't matter how many feet, and eventually miles, I put behind me. I can't escape what I'm running from, because it's the memories and they live inside me.

CHAPTER FOUR

My legs ache with tiredness and I finally stop, leaning my bike against the outside of a bookstore. The name etched into the glass front says That's My Story and in smaller font beneath says *and I'm sticking to it*. I smile to myself, thinking it's a cute name and catchphrase for a bookstore. An old fashioned sign hangs on the door saying OPEN.

I push it open and step inside. The smell of books—crisp paper and ink—hits my nostrils. I've never been a huge reader, but I'm not opposed to it.

The store is old and inviting, and while I see newer books, it has the musky scent of older volumes as well.

"Whatcha lookin' for, missy?"

I jump at the sound of the voice and turn, spotting an older gentleman behind an ancient looking register.

Suspenders wrap around his shoulders and he sports a handlebar mustache.

"Uh ... not sure," I reply.

"Well, have a look around and if you need help let me know."

I raise a brow, because he looks ancient and I'm pretty sure I'm the one who should be offering him help.

I stroll through the aisles, gliding my fingers over spines and reading the titles. I don't know what compelled me here, but something about the store feels *right* in an unexplainable way.

I pull a random book off a shelf, flipping through the pages before I replace it.

I pause in front of a book titled *Moons*. My heart beats faster as I grab it. The cover is speckled with stars with a large moon in the center that wraps around onto the spine. When I open it I realize it has details and information on all the known moons in the universe. A part of me wants to put the book back, but it feels like too big of a coincidence. I've never been a believer in the dead speaking from beyond, but it feels like Luna wanted me to find this.

Tucking the book under my arm, I stroll through the small store a few more minutes before I make my purchase.

"See you again," the older man says with a smile, handing me the bag.

"Mhmm," I hum, doubting I'll be back.

Outside, I tuck the bag into my basket and ride a little further until I spot a café. I run inside and purchase a smoothie, deciding if I don't head home now my parents will have the entire state's police force searching for me.

The ride home feels like it takes forever, but I know it can't be more than twenty minutes. They'll be mad at me for being gone so long, but they understand the need to get away as well. We're all trying to escape the pain, like we can outrun it.

I put in the code for the garage door and it whirls as it goes up. I tuck my bike back against the wall, noticing someone picked up the box I knocked over.

It's labeled with *Photos* on the side in my dad's messy handwriting. Grabbing a knife left on another box I open it up, searching for what I broke.

I find it at the bottom, a framed photo of Luna and me. I'm in my cheer uniform, smiling wide for the camera with my arm wrapped around her. She's smiling, but her eyes are sad. There's a crack now in the glass, cutting between the two of us, shattering the connection. It's one of the last photos we took together besides the random selfie. I remember the day well. It was the final football game of the season. I begged her to come since she hadn't attended a single game. After all my pestering she reluctantly agreed. I had no idea at the time that she avoided the games because of the group of girls in her eighth grade class who attended every single one. I didn't know they bullied her. I didn't know I needed to protect her. And when I smiled at the camera, hugging my sister to my side, I had no idea only a few short months later I'd be saying goodbye forever.

The door opens and in my startle I drop the frame on the floor. It shatters further.

"You can't run off like that," my mom scolds,

descending the stairs into the garage. She bends and picks up the frame. The broken glass has damaged the photo beneath. Her fingers hover above Luna's now distorted face. "I loved this photo."

I brush past her. "I hate it." The words are whispered under my breath. She doesn't hear me as she picks up the small pieces of glass from the floor and removes the photo from the frame.

I pause with my hand on the door, feeling anger rise inside me, because that stupid frame can be replaced, but not my sister's life.

With a shake of my head I enter the house and head to the kitchen. French toast is stacked on a plate and my dad is nowhere to be seen. I grab some for myself despite not feeling hungry.

"You left these in your basket, Vi." My mom breezes into the pristine kitchen and deposits my green smoothie and the bag with my book on the table beside me.

"Thanks."

She looks at me sadly, nibbling on her bottom lip as she debates saying something.

After a long moment she shakes her head and leaves.

Avoidance. It's the one thing the three of us have in common right now.

I wanted to talk about Luna's death in the beginning, about my grief, and the burden of feeling like it was my fault. That I should've known. But neither of them could take it. Now, as the months pass and our grief progresses none of us knows how to broach the subject.

It's a difficult thing having someone you love be there one second and gone the next.

Death is a natural part of life, but there's nothing normal about a fourteen-year-old girl hanging herself in her closet. I think for us, because her death was her *choice* it's harder to accept. Not because suicide is wrong, but because we should've known. Seen the signs. Done *something*. Anything.

But that's the thing about depression and suicide. It's a silent killer, slowly sucking the life out of someone you love. You don't realize until it's too late, and by then there's nothing you can do.

CHAPTER FIVE

AFTER UNPACKING FOR SEVERAL DAYS STRAIGHT, THE house comes together. It still doesn't feel like a home to me, it's missing the sound of laughter and happiness radiating from the walls, but it'll do.

There are two weeks until my senior year starts and my schedule arrives in the mail. Since I knew I wasn't going to cheer, I signed up for classes that would give me dual credit. I figured I might as well get a jump on the whole college thing.

"Is that your schedule?" Mom questions, blowing her bangs out of her eyes as she vigorously stirs cake batter. It's my dad's birthday, and even though he's not supposed to start work until Monday he had to run to the office.

"Yeah." I hold it out to her and she takes it, looking it over.

"You're going to be busy." She passes it back to me. "I know you can handle it."

She gives me an encouraging smile and I'm thankful for it, because I, on the other hand, am not sure I can do this. But I sure as hell need the distraction.

"Need any help?" I lean my hip against the counter and swipe my finger into the batter, taking a lick.

She swats my hand away playfully and my heart clenches, because I haven't shared many of these carefree moments with either of my parents lately. It's like we feel like it's wrong to be happy or live our lives because Luna can't.

"You're always welcome to help. Grab an apron."

She points to the pantry door and I open it up, grabbing the yellow one with sunflowers and tying it around my body.

I turn on some music and my mom and I dance around the kitchen as we bake the cake and frost it. I pour on too many sprinkles according to her, but I mean, there's no such thing.

She slides the cake cover over top and pulls me into a hug. "We did good, kiddo."

I wrap my arms around her middle, hugging her tight. I might be seventeen, nearly eighteen, but you're never too old to need a hug from your mom. She lays her head over top of mine. I soak in the moment, needing the comfort of human touch far more than I realized.

She pulls away, but keeps her hands on my shoulders. "You're a strong, beautiful, intelligent, fantastically brilliant daughter. I know I don't say it enough, but you are."

Tears shimmer in her eyes and she turns, wiping them away. "I'm going to freshen up before your dad gets home."

With those parting words she heads upstairs to the master bedroom.

I know she's probably going to cry about Luna. I wish she'd let me be there for her, each a shoulder for the other to cry on, but we all keep acting like it's not happening and the grief doesn't exist.

I wipe down the counters and hang up the apron.

I don't have any idea what to do with my time until school starts. I have no friends and my family is falling apart.

Slipping on my flip-flops I kicked off when we started baking, I slide open the back door and head down the deck steps and to the meadow beyond. The grass is overgrown, and maybe I should be scared of snakes, but I'm not.

Fear is an illusion. The only true thing in life we have to fear is ourselves.

Beyond the meadow there's forest. One day maybe it'll be turned into housing, but for now I love that there's land back there.

I find a spot and lay down in the swaying grass, staring up at the clouds above.

The heat from the sun warms my skin, but I don't mind it. It's probably not smart of me to be lying here staring straight up at the sky, but I've done far worse things in the past.

"Cumulus."

I jolt at the sound of the male voice and sit up, turning to find the guy I spotted nights ago with the telescope next door. Up close he definitely looks to be my age. He's tall and lanky with freckles speckled across his nose. He pushes his glasses up. I want to know what color his eyes are, but he's not looking at me. His gaze is focused intently on the sky above.

"W-What?" I stutter, taken off guard.

"Cumulus." This time he points to the clouds. "We always get the boring ones."

"You're my neighbor," I blurt. "I'm Violet."

His head angles down slightly toward me where I sit on the ground, but quickly darts back to the sky before he even makes eye contact. "I know. I've watched you."

Not creepy at all.

"You've watched me?"

"I've watched you watching me."

He has a fair point. I've spotted him at his telescope a few more times since the first, and my bedroom window that overlooks the side of his house is right across from a window in his room.

"Do you have a name?"

Those eyes of his that I still don't know the color of dart over my face quickly and away. "Finn."

"Can you help me up, Finn?" I hold out my hand.

Once again his eyes dash around, like they don't want to land on one particular thing, and he starts to walk away.

My lips part as I watch him walk back to his house. He doesn't look back, not until the door closes behind him.

When he sees me watching the blinds are promptly shut.

The whole exchange was weird, but I figure something

is up with him physically since I've seen him with a service dog, walking it around the neighborhood.

Maybe he's blind.

Then how could he see the clouds, dipshit? And I'm pretty sure blind people don't stare longingly into a telescope every night.

I know there's no point in trying to puzzle out my strange new neighbor, but I am insanely curious about him.

I stand up and dust grass from my legs and clothes before I return to the house.

Hours later, my dad arrives home and since it's his birthday we order in Italian food from a place down the road we got a flyer for in the mail.

My mom and I sing him happy birthday and he blows out forty-seven candles. I insisted there be forty-seven exactly. I don't half ass birthdays.

After we each eat a slice of cake we go our separate ways.

When I sneak out my window at midnight my eyes immediately find Finn standing by his telescope.

I wave.

There's a flash of something white and I swear he smiles, but it's gone too quickly for me to be sure.

He turns his attention to his telescope and I stretch out on the sloping roof to take in the stars.

It's not lost on me that we're looking at the exact same universe from very different perspectives.

CHAPTER SIX

I'VE BECOME WELL ACQUAINTED WITH THE neighborhood and the surrounding city and shops.

Surprisingly, I actually like it here. It's picturesque, the kind of town you'd see on the front of a postcard. I think if we'd moved here for any other reason besides pure escapism I would love it even more. For now, I can't help looking around and thinking about *why* we're here.

I pick up a sandwich and smoothie from the place I came to the day after I arrived. Sweet Greens has become a favorite of mine and I ride my bike there a few times a week to grab lunch. Biking back toward the house the wind stirs my long hair around my shoulders. I should probably cut it, but I like it how it is.

There's a park not far from the neighborhood and I head over there to eat my lunch. I like being outside, I always have. There's a calmness I find in nature that I can't discover anywhere else.

Hopping off my bike I wheel it over to a bench beneath a shaded willow tree. A creek trickles by it. The sound is peaceful and I enjoy watching the fish and turtles.

The frogs, not so much. The first time I stopped here one jumped on my foot. I shrieked and kicked my leg, which sent the poor frog flying.

I grab the paper bag with my sandwich and my cup of green smoothie—full of all those healthy things we need, but hate to eat.

I take a sip and pull out my sandwich. The park is abuzz with life. Children laughing, teens enjoying the last of summer, college kids studying, people jogging, dogs barking, and even a chaotic soccer game between a couple of guys.

It's all so idyllic.

I eat my sandwich, watching the chaos of life around me. Everyone seems to be moving so fast while I'm so still.

Normally, I look forward to the start of school. Friends return from summer vacations to the tropics and it's the start of football season and house parties on weekends. But this year, the thought of those things only leaves me feeling disgusted with a rotten taste in my mouth.

I still haven't heard from a single one of my friends in the weeks since I arrived here. I'm not surprised, but that doesn't mean it doesn't hurt. It's a reminder of how superficial everything about my life was before.

At least I've gotten used to not having friends. It'll make starting a new school, knowing absolutely no one, a lot easier. I'm not interested in making friends anyway. I just want to graduate and get it over with.

Finished with my sandwich and drink, I toss the trash in the bin by the bench and get up, straddling my bike.

I pause, spotting a boy with his dog in the distance.

Finn.

I'm strangely drawn to the boy next door and I think it's because his endearing awkwardness reminds me of my sister. She was always shy and had trouble keeping eye contact just like he does. There's more in common between them than that, but it's not the only reason I feel pulled into his orbit.

In those brief glances we exchange most nights, I can't quite see his expression or any details of any sort, but there's this mutual understanding of loneliness.

I suppose I could be projecting it, searching desperately for any sort of connection, something to keep me tethered to reality.

I know I should get on my bike and ride home, leave him and his dog alone, but my legs have a mind of their own and I guide my bike over to him and his pooch.

"Hi." My voice is soft, hesitant.

He's sitting, some kind of book propped in his lap. His head is bent over it, his messy dark hair obscuring his face. His body stiffens at the sound of my voice and he doesn't look up. From his posture I *know* he recognizes my voice.

"It's Violet."

No reply.

"I like your dog. He seems nice." His service dog, a yellow lab, pants beside him wearing his blue vest. There's a portable water bowl in front of the dog and a half empty bottle of water lying beside Finn's leg. "What's his name?"

Finn taps his foot restlessly, and his finger is paused on the last word he read. It almost looks like he's holding his breath.

The last thing I want to do is make him feel uncomfortable and he's showing all the classic signs that say *go away.* Exhaling a breath I say, "I'm heading home. Just wanted to say hi."

I start to wheel my bike away, in the direction of the sidewalk, when he finally speaks.

"Jack."

The dog's name.

I don't turn around. I don't say anything at all. Just continue on my way, but there's no denying the smile on my face.

CHAPTER SEVEN

My alarm goes off at six o' clock and I immediately silence it with a groan. I don't know anyone, at least any sane person, who enjoys the sound of an alarm jarring them from sleep.

I roll over, clutching one of my gray pillows to my chest.

The last thing I want to do is get up and ready for school, but I have no choice.

Shoving the blankets off of me I force my body out of bed and into the bathroom, pouting the whole way.

I don't really care much what I look like, I'm not going to make friends or socialize, but I do apply some mascara to my lashes and a clear gloss to my lips. For clothes, I pick out a pair of ripped jean shorts and a blousy top with flowers on it.

Slipping my feet into a pair of flip-flops my mom yells up the stairs, "Breakfast is ready, Vi!"

Looking in the floor length mirror in the corner of my room I tilt my head at my reflection. "Well, here goes nothing," I mutter to myself.

I grab my backpack from the floor and sling it over my shoulder, switching off the lights as I leave my room.

Dropping my bag by the garage door I meet my parents in the kitchen. Both already sit at the kitchen table, eating freshly made waffles and drinking coffee.

My heart pangs. Every year since I started school my mom has always made waffles for the first day. For some reason I thought this year would be different.

I pull out a chair, sitting across from my mom and beside my dad.

"This looks delicious, Mom." I drench my waffles in syrup and my stomach growls.

She beams as I cut into them.

"I want to get a picture of you before you leave," she warns, pointing a finger at me. "Don't even think about dining and dashing."

"Mom," I grind. "I'm seventeen, a senior. I hardly think this is necessary."

My dad lowers the newspaper he was reading. "We have a picture of you girls—" He jolts, shaking his head. "We have pictures of you on every first day of school you've had. Don't buck tradition now, kiddo."

I nod as we all try to ignore his slip.

Luna would've been starting her freshman year today.

She'll never go to homecoming, or prom, graduate, go to college, or fall in love.

Her life is forever trapped in fourteen too short years.

Nothing else is said for the rest of the meal and when I finish I clean my plate before grabbing my lunch and stuffing it in my backpack. I swing the bag around my shoulders and turn toward my mom. "Where do you want to take the picture, Mom?"

Her eyes are distant as she bends over the sink, scrubbing her already clean plate. "Huh?"

"The picture. Where do you want to take it?"

Shaking her head she lets go of the plate and it clangs against the stainless steel bottom of the sink.

"Uh..." She wipes her hands down the front of her jeans. "The front porch is fine."

"Remember to smile," my dad jokes with a wink. I know he's trying to lighten the mood, but it's not working, especially since I can see the sadness clouding his eyes.

I follow my mom outside and pose for photos on the front porch.

At the house next door I hear a commotion and look over to see Finn and his dog, Jack, heading to a car parked in the driveway. A woman I assume is his mother, small framed with the same dark hair, rushes after him and seems to be asking him a list of things to which he keeps nodding. Our houses are close enough together that I can see his expression clearly and he's frustrated. When she keeps going he finally throws his hands in the air, anger contorting his face. He grabs the driver's door and gets inside, backing out so fast she has to jerk away from the car or get run over. She turns, watching his car drive away with worry in her eyes.

"Okay, I think that's enough." Mom bends her head, going through the, I'm sure hundreds, of photos she's taken.

"Good luck today, kiddo." Dad kisses the top of my head. "I can drop you off on my way if you need me to?"

I shake my head. "I'm going to bike over."

"You sure?" He raises a brow in question. "I'm happy to take you."

"I can pick you up if that's what you're worried about," my mom pipes in, putting her phone in her pocket.

"No, really, I'm fine. I like riding my bike. It clears my head."

They let it go and I grab my bike from the garage, waving goodbye as they watch me leave.

The school is only about five miles away and I've already been a few times, checking out where all my classes are and getting a feel for it.

The school is beautiful, two levels and spanning a wide expanse. A large, multi-level set of concrete stairs leads to the front. It has columns and ivy growing up the brick exterior. Windows cover the front, more windows than I've ever seen any school have. The grounds are beautiful too. The front of the school boasts a large yard, and from my exploring I know the cafeteria is near the back with an attached, senior only, garden with tables for eating.

When I reach the grounds I'm blown away by how

packed the parking lot is already and all the teens dotting the stairs and expansive yard before the final bell rings.

I park my bike in the designated area, pulling the lock from my backpack and securing it in place.

My hands shake slightly at my sides as I head for the massive front doors and I fold them into fists hoping no one will notice my nerves.

Inside, my flip-flops smack against the black and white marble flooring. This is definitely a rich people's school, and while my family isn't poor we're definitely not wealthy on this scale either. A few years ago the school used to require uniforms, but finally did away with that rule.

I have my schedule memorized and I head to my first class, Advanced English, and sit outside the door. The bell will be ringing any minute, signaling the masses to herd into classrooms, but even if it wasn't I'd still come here to wait. The idea of watching people greet their friends, laughing and squealing, isn't appealing when I have no one. I don't *need* friends, but that doesn't mean I don't want them. Does anyone like feeling alone? But I also refuse to fall into the crowd I was in before.

Not that they were bad, but they—*we*—weren't exactly nice to everyone.

And it was girls like that, like *me*, who bullied my sister to the point she saw no choice but to take her own life.

I won't be that girl anymore. Not just for Luna, but for me. I don't want people to remember me because I was popular, cliquish, and spiteful. There's more to life than being the center of attention.

A teacher walks down the hall and he stops, appraising

me with a tilt of his head. "I don't know of any sane student who hangs outside my classroom. Haven't you heard? I'm the mean one."

I look up at him. He's older, probably in his fifties, with graying hair cut short. His eyes are wrinkled and his lips downturned, but despite his words about being mean there's mischief in his eyes. He pulls a pair of keys from his pockets and twirls them around.

"I just moved here. Must've missed the memo." I shrug and stand up as he unlocks the door. It swings open and he reaches inside, flicking the light on before motioning me ahead.

"I don't think hiding in the English hallway is the way to make friends," he remarks with a raised brow, standing over his cluttered desk. I quirk a brow, wondering how it's possibly so messy and school hasn't even started.

"I'm not looking to make friends."

He fights a smile and taps his forehead. "Smart girl. Sit wherever." He motions to the desks. They're designed for two people to sit at them at a time and all laid out in a haphazard pattern.

I pick a seat in the corner where I'll have the least amount of contact with anyone except for whoever sits beside me. He chuckles when he sees the seat I've chosen.

He sits down behind his desk and shuffles some papers.

I sit there, with nothing to do, because even though I could pull my phone out I don't have anyone to talk to and I'm not one to play games.

After a moment he clears his throat. "Can you place a

copy of those in front of each seat?" He points to piles and piles of *Les Miserables* stacked beneath the chalkboard.

"Yeah."

I push away from the table, the metal legs of the chair scraping across the tile floors. Two windows on the left of the room look out toward a basketball court and tennis courts beyond it. I pick up as many books as I can carry at a time and start setting them down.

"What's your name?" He picks up a pen, uncapping it. "I'll mark you on my roster."

"Violet Page."

He checks me off on his list and I've placed the last book down when I hurry to my chair to sit down before my classmates start pouring in.

I finger the worn book in front of me. It says on the cover it's the abridged version, but even still it looks massive.

The seats fill up and when the final bell rings the teacher, Mr. Rochester according to my schedule—which is ironic, because *Jane Eyre*—stands and slams the door closed causing us to jump. We all jump again when a body slams into the closed door.

Mr. Rochester smiles at the guy through the window and wags his finger. "The bell rang. No admittance. Be here on time or get locked out."

The guy groans on the other side of the glass window and opens his mouth to argue but Mr. Rochester lowers the blinds and flips them closed.

Walking away from the door he paces between the

tables. A girl took the seat beside me, her bag resting precariously on the edge.

Mr. Rochester stops beside it and gives it a slight nudge, knocking it to the ground. Her jaw drops and she scoffs as she grabs it, this time draping the straps over the back of her chair.

"By now, you've probably heard about me from previous upperclassmen. That I'm loud. I cuss. I expect too much and I'll fail your paper on the spot if you use the Goddamn word *you* in an essay. All of that is true. I'm here to teach you. Make you better. Prepare you for college and the beast called life that will fucking devour you if you're not ready. I will not coddle you. This class is worth a college credit and I expect you to act like it. If you don't finish a paper on time, you fail. You give me excuses, you fail. Own your mistakes." He passes behind my table and around. "If you don't think you can handle it, get out now." He pauses in the middle of the floor, spreading his arms. When no one moves, he smirks. "I'm not kidding. If you don't think you can cut it, now's your chance to leave. Head to the office and request a transfer. I don't care today, but don't decide to stick around today and then waste my fucking time."

My jaw drops when three students grab their stuff and actually walk out the door.

He raises a brow, making eye contact with each and every one of us. "Anyone else?"

One more person leaves.

He clasps his hands and smirks. "Last chance."

No one moves. I don't think anyone even dares to breathe. I look beside me and see that the girl who was beside me has fled.

Mr. Rochester tilts his head to the side. "I like to get rid of the weak. Your classmates who left? If this was the Middle Ages they're the ones who would starve to death because they're not willing to put in any effort. I commend you all for choosing to stay. You'll do far better in life than those weaklings. You see, I'm really not all that mean of a teacher." He walks around again. "I just expect you to perform at your utmost best. My classroom isn't for half-assers. You're here to learn. There's a book in front of each of you. *Les Miserables* is our first read this year. We'll be studying it for the next several weeks. You'll be required to write an essay and as you read there will be pop quizzes. If you think you can SparkNotes this shit," he picks up the book from in front of a guy, slamming it back down on the tabletop and causing him to jump, "then you're sorely mistaken. I eat kids like you for breakfast. Do the work. Reap the rewards. And maybe, if I feel so inclined, I'll write a college recommendation letter for you. And trust me, you want that. I have clout and pull with *a lot* of schools. If any of you think you're getting into Harvard or wherever your Ivy League dreams take you, without me, you're wrong. Just as easily as I can give you a recommendation I can also put in a word about what a sniveling bitch you are."

I swear the girl across from me looks ready to faint.

Mr. Rochester swirls his finger through the air. "Start

reading, and I assure you if any of you idiots have a question I will personally escort you from my classroom. Reading a book shouldn't require questions. You just fucking do it."

Everyone sits stunned as he finally pulls out his desk chair.

I flip open the book and a moment later jump when he claps his hands loudly. "Are you all deaf? Stop staring at me and open the fucking book."

"Oh my God," someone whispers, "I think I should've left with the others."

"Then leave," Mr. Rochester responds, not looking up from the paper he's reading. "I'm not here to wipe your nose or clean your ass."

The girl huffs but opens the book and begins to read. I slide my eyes to Mr. Rochester and find him smirking at whatever he's reading, but I have a feeling that's not his source of amusement.

Class ends after ninety minutes and everyone races to escape.

I linger behind, clutching the worn copy of *Les Miserables* to my chest. "You like making kids shit their pants, don't you?"

Laughter bursts out of Mr. Rochester. "Best part about this job is scaring teenagers into not being dicks—at least in my classroom."

"Well, see you Wednesday."

He nods after me and I head to my next class, Calculus. Math is my least favorite subject, so my feet drag down the hall. I reach the classroom and take a seat near the back of one of the neatly lined rows.

When everyone's arrived, and the bell has rung, the teacher passes out textbooks.

Mrs. Kennedy is probably in her forties with round tired eyes hidden behind a pair of even rounder glasses. She dresses way too frumpy for her age and is so short I wonder how she can possibly drive a car. Maybe she doesn't for all I know.

The class is spent going over her syllabus and what she expects from us.

I'm wondering if I shouldn't raise my hand and just tell her to fail me now, because passing doesn't seem like a likely possibility and it's only the first day.

Before class ends she passes out a worksheet with five equations and asks us to solve them before we return to day one classes on Wednesday. She wants to evaluate where we're at and I know she isn't going to like where I stand.

The bell rings, signaling the start of lunch for seniors.

Everyone floods the halls, excitement in the air for a short break. Students rush by me, eager to meet up with friends, while I mosey slowly along.

My whole, I don't need friends things, hasn't bothered me until this moment.

I've never not had anyone to sit with at lunch. The idea of facing a crowd of seniors and not having anywhere I belong kind of sucks.

But I square my shoulders and plow on. I pass through the crowded cafeteria and breeze outside to one of the tables out there. It's empty and I slap my backpack down on the table, claiming it as mine. I sit down on the hard metal bench and dig my lunch out of my backpack.

My eyes stray to the windows, at all the chattering teens catching up from their morning classes.

It's all so normal.

There are fewer people outside, for which I'm grateful. I can easily tune out the chatter and eat my sandwich.

The door to the patio opens again and I look up, spotting Finn walking out with Jack.

He doesn't notice me, focused solely on getting Jack in the grass for a potty break.

After Jack does his business he sits down on the ground with his back against the brick exterior of the building, stretching his legs into the grass. He opens his backpack and yanks out a brown paper bag lunch sack. As he's zipping his backpack he catches me staring and I look away hastily.

My cheeks sting with embarrassment at getting caught.

"Why were you looking at that weirdo?" A girl from the table beside mine, sitting with three other friends, speaks to me.

"Huh?" I tuck a piece of hair behind my ear.

She nods her head in Finn's direction. "Finnley Crawford is the strangest guy I've ever seen. I'd stay away from him if I were you."

I look at Finn over my shoulder. He picks off a piece of what I assume is turkey from his sandwich and gives it to Jack, who takes it delicately from his fingers. Finn cracks a small smile and rubs the dog's head.

"I mean, look at him. I heard he has that dog because of

anger issues. Apparently he punched a teacher in middle school because the teacher looked at him funny." She shudders, the gesture not disturbing a perfect blonde hair on her head. I'm pretty sure it's hair sprayed so hard that it'll never move again.

"Have you ever spoken to him?" I counter, cocking my head to the side.

She crinkles her bunny nose. "No," she scoffs, "why would I?"

I stand up, grabbing my stuff. "Just because someone is different than you, or you don't understand them, doesn't mean they're beneath you."

Her jaw drops. "Excuse me?"

"You heard me." I walk away, and I hear her whispering to her friends behind me. I've probably just slapped a giant target across my back, but I don't care.

Kids didn't understand my sister. They ignored her and ostracized her. They mocked her and belittled her.

They thought their words didn't matter.

"Hi, Finn."

I stop in front of him. His black boots are centimeters away from the tips of my flip-flops. His head is bowed slightly and he lets Jack lick his fingers.

"Do you mind if I sit with you?"

He scratches Jack's ears and jerks his eyes toward me and away. "Why?"

"Those girls aren't very nice and I don't know anyone. I just moved here."

I know he knows I've just moved, but it feels necessary to remind him.

"Why?" he repeats.

"Because you're sitting alone and I'm sitting alone, and maybe if we sit together we won't be so alone then?" I squint against the sun and he tilts his face toward me.

He's good-looking, but in a quirky way, where his mouth is too large for his face and his nose too pointy but it suits him. In fact, I'm pretty sure if he wasn't different girls would fawn all over him. He has the broody, tortured, artist or poet vibe down.

"Fine."

I know it's all the answer I'm going to get. I sit down beside him, careful to keep a few feet between us when I notice him stiffen.

"Thanks for letting me sit with you."

He grunts in response.

His body is angled away from mine and toward his dog. His posture is rigid and I should probably just leave, but I feel like I'm right where I'm supposed to be.

"You like stars, huh?"

I don't expect an answer but out of my peripheral I notice him nod.

"I do too." I pick off a piece of sandwich and hand it to Finn. He promptly gives it to Jack. "There's a whole other world out there," I muse.

He rubs his lips together and pushes his glasses up his nose.

"Infinite possibilities." He speaks the words softly, carefully.

The bell rings, dismissing us to a short free period. I

pick up my trash and take Finn's too, tossing it in the bin. "Can I sit with you tomorrow?"

He's picking grass off of Jack's vest and I know he's heard me, just buying time to decide what he wants to say. "I guess."

I smile.

Victory.

CHAPTER EIGHT

I ONLY MANAGE TO FINISH ONE CALCULUS EQUATION before the bell rings and I'm sent to my next class, Physics. It's the one class I'll have every day. I couldn't luck out with having an elective every day. No, I'm stuck with *Physics*. That just seems like pure cruelty on behalf of whoever set up my schedule.

I race down the hall and up the stairs toward the science department. The Physics classroom is as far as humanly possible from the one my free period is in.

I get some strange looks as I race down the halls, but I don't care.

Just before the bell rings I make it inside the room and scan the lab tables for an empty seat.

All are full until I notice one in the very back corner.

Finn leans against the wall, his head ducked down, with the only empty seat beside him.

"Please, take a seat," the teacher clips at me, pointing to the stool.

I sigh and walk between the aisles, feeling the eyes of my fellow classmates on me. I pull out the metal stool and it clangs against the floor. I shrug my backpack off and place it on the floor, leaning against the large lab counter, before I sit down.

Finn shifts away, it's not like he can get much farther, and Jack lies on the floor between us.

"I'm Mr. Lambert," the teacher says in a curt tone, grabbing a stack of sheets and handing it to the first kid. "Pass these among yourselves and we'll go over the requirements I have for you in my classroom. For example..." He pauses and his eyes stop on me. "This young lady here, Miss?"

"Uh..." Every eye in the room turns to me and I hear Finn squeak the chair some more. "Page. Violet Page."

"Miss Page is wearing flip-flops. Flip-flops are not permitted on lab days. I will notify you of this prior to lab days, but if you fail to show up dressed properly with legs and feet covered, you will be given a fail grade."

Unlike Mr. Rochester there's no secret laughter in this guy's eyes. With a thick mustache and out of control hair and eyebrows he definitely looks the part of the mad scientist.

Eventually the papers make it to our table and I grab one, passing it to Finn. He doesn't take it so I lay it in front of him before grabbing one for myself and leaving the stack on the end of the table since there's no one left to give them to.

Up front Mr. Lambert reads over the list of rules, regulations, and his own personal quirks and choices for his classroom.

Namely, no chewing gum, no drinking water, and no snacks.

The rest of the class is spent going over his plans for our next class and passing out textbooks and workbooks. The first day of school is always so vastly boring to me. There are so many rules to go over and expectations, that generally not much work is started. So far Mr. Rochester is the only one who's gotten straight to work, and while nobody else might, I appreciate him for that.

Beside me, Finn spends the period squirming in his chair and tugging on his collar, looking generally uncomfortable.

If I could move to another table I would, not because he's bothering me, but because I get the distinct sense that my closeness is bothering *him*.

Mr. Lambert finishes speaking and looks at the large clock above the door. "Ten minutes are left. Talk *quietly* amongst yourselves."

The room immediately bursts into robust chatter and Finn covers his ears with his hands, resting his elbows on the black counter in front of us. I bite my lip, knowing the sound of so many voices is bothering him, but I don't know how to make it better without upsetting him. The last thing

I want to do is invade his space and make him more uncomfortable.

"I said *quietly*," Mr. Lambert repeats.

The voices soften, but Finn keeps his ears covered.

Jack stands up, rubbing his body against Finn's restless legs that bounce against the footrest of the stool.

Finn calms some, but doesn't remove his hands from his ears.

I shoot my hand in the air and the movement must catch Mr. Lambert's eyes because he looks up from the book he's reading and removes his reading glasses. "Yes?" He arches a brow.

"Would it be okay if Finn and I go to the library for the last few minutes?"

His eyes slide from me to my table partner and he shrugs. "You're dismissed."

I turn to Finn, but I can't catch his eye.

"Library," I mouth. "We can go to the library."

He nods eagerly, thankfully, and I pick up my backpack and his. Finn grabs Jack's leash and hauls ass out of the classroom, toward the lower level library. I struggle to keep up with his long-legged stride.

"Finn," I plead, practically running to keep up. "Slow down. I have little legs compared to you."

He listens and slows. When I catch up with him he takes his backpack from me and slips it on.

In record time we make it to the library. I visited it briefly when I came to look around, and it's certainly impressive, with high ceilings that sport a mural of cherubs and look like something you're more likely to see in a church in Greece than an American high school, dark wood shelves, and chandeliers. There are tables dotted through the whole library along with some leather club chairs, perfect for reading.

I follow Finn to a table and he pulls out a chair. He collapses into it, letting out a heavy breath. Jack rests his head on Finn's leg, looking on with worried eyes at his charge.

I slide the chair out across from Finn and sit down, placing my backpack on the table between us.

Before my butt touches the seat Finn startles me with a question.

"Why are you nice to me?"

I think it's the first full sentence he's ever spoken to me.

"Why wouldn't I be nice to you?" I scoot my backpack to the other side of the table and clasp my fingers together, laying them on the table.

He wets his lips, looking at the knotted wood table. "No one else is."

"Their loss, then."

His eyes meet mine briefly, and the deep blue color of them reminds me of the midnight blue night sky. "You feel sorry for me."

"I don't." I feel the furthest thing from sorry for him.

"They're afraid of me," he murmurs, the confession dripping from his tongue with the displeasure of something sour tasting.

"They don't understand you."

"And you do?" He counters.

"You're just like everyone else."

A humorless laugh bursts from his lips. "I'm not. I wish I was, but I'm not."

Before I can say anything else, he gets up and I watch him and Jack head for the exit.

I don't follow. I know he doesn't want me to.

CHAPTER NINE

The first week of school ends and it feels like a weight has been lifted off my chest. My new school isn't bad, but somehow I've become a social pariah by speaking to Finn and sitting with him at lunch. That fact doesn't sit well with me.

Not because I want people to like me, but their unnecessary judgment clouds my vision with red.

Finn hasn't uttered one word to me since the library incident. I'm following his lead and not saying anything, though we do sit outside together at lunch, side by side with a few empty feet between us. Sometimes it's only the grass separating us. Other times it's Jack who will sit between us.

I park my bike outside the garage, and enter the code to get inside.

I can't help noticing Finn's car is already parked in front of his house.

Inside, I find a note from my mom saying she's run to the grocery store and will be back in an hour.

I grab a soda from the refrigerator and head up to my room.

Will Ferret rustles in his cage, poking his head up when he sees me.

I grin and set my drink down. "Hey, buddy." I open his cage and he runs to me to be held. I gather him in my arms and kiss the top of his soft head. I kick my door closed and set him down so he can run around.

He circles between my legs and I giggle.

He follows me as I open my window and slip outside onto the roof. "I'll be back in a minute, Will. I need a breath of fresh air."

The little ferret looks hardly appeased by my words, but finds one of his toys on the floor and starts playing.

I inhale a lungful of air, feeling it fill up my chest, before I slowly exhale it.

"Approximately one-hundred and seventy-five days to go."

I don't know why I think graduating will magically fix everything. Logically, I know it won't, but I need some-thing to hope for.

Hope is the only thing keeping my heart beating right now.

After several minutes I climb back inside and play with Will for a while before I start on homework.

"Vi! I'm home!" My mom yells from downstairs and the garage door alarm chirps.

"Doing homework!"

Luckily, I don't have much to do. Thanks to not doing cheerleading I have a lot more free time and I've spent most of it staying ahead on the piles of homework the teachers have assigned.

It only takes me an hour to finish and I carefully put everything away.

My room is perfectly neat and tidy. It never was before, but I can't seem to thrive in chaos like I once did.

Heading down the stairs I find my mom in the kitchen, ingredients spread across the counter as she prepares to make dinner.

Shoving my hands into my back pockets I rock back and forth on the heels of my feet. "Can I help you with anything?"

"Oh, yes." She blows out a frazzled breath. "Can you get some water boiling in the pot?"

I nod and walk over to the sink, turning it on to the hottest setting. I dig out the biggest pot we own and fill it up, sticking it on the stove and turning it on.

"Are you making the sauce from scratch?" I arch a brow at my mom who's currently piling tomatoes into a food processor.

Her shoulders sag. "Y-Yes." She bites her lip, looking unsure of herself. "Is that dumb? I thought I'd try something different."

"No, I think it's great," I rush to assure her. "I was kind of in disbelief."

"It's probably silly," she sighs, adding garlic and then basil. "You want to roll out the meatballs?"

"Sure."

We work together and it doesn't take long to get everything wrapped up. It's after five o' clock and my dad should be home by six at the latest.

Just as we're plating the spaghetti and meatballs my dad arrives home.

"Ladies," he calls, "something smells delicious." He enters the kitchen tugging at his tie. It's always funny seeing my dad dressed in a shirt and tie. He looks like he belongs in shorts with a Dad joke shirt, a beer in one hand, and standing over a grill. He hates the dressy clothes he has to wear and always changes first thing. He kisses my cheek, then my mom's, and backs away pointing at us. "I'm going to change and I'll be right down."

My mom lets out a soft giggle when he leaves.

"What?" I prompt.

She shakes her head. "I was just thinking about how it's a miracle he doesn't rip his clothes off when he gets home since he hates them so much. Maybe once you're gone to college he will. I won't mind."

A disgusted expression contorts my face. "Oh, ew, *Mom*. No." I shake my head back and forth rapidly. "I don't need that visual."

"You asked."

She has a point.

We set everything on the table, and thankfully there's no more talk of stripping clothes, and by the time the two of us sit down my dad rejoins us.

"Better?" My mom asks him with a slight laugh.

"Much," he replies. "This looks amazing, girls. You've outdone yourselves."

"Mom made the sauce from scratch." I flash her a smile, ignoring the pain in my chest. It's moments like these when I'm reminded the most of the person missing. It's not supposed to be three of us, and seeing the empty spot at the table makes my heart ache with sadness.

I spoon some spaghetti onto my plate and grab a piece of garlic bread, digging in.

"How's school going?" Dad asks, waiting for my reply before he takes a bite.

"Uh ... it's school." I press my lips together, not sure what else to say.

"Yeah, but how are the teachers? Your classes?"

"It's all fine."

His lips downturn and I know he's not happy with my less than enthusiastic response.

But I don't feel like explaining that it's not the school. It's *me*. I'm lost and I can't find myself. I call out, but my voice echoes into an endless void.

My mom asks him about his day at work and the conversation moves from me.

"We should do something as a family this weekend," my mom urges with a smile, nudging me back into the conversation.

"Like what?" I'm not being surly, just genuinely curious.

"There are all kinds of historical tours," my dad pipes

in enthusiastically. My mom and I look at him in disbelief and he chuckles. "Or not."

"What about the mall?" My mom asks me, and I know she's trying hard.

For months we've all been trapped in our heads, drowning in guilt and grief, but it's time to pull ourselves out. Start living again. The only thing is, I'm not sure I'm ready.

But I owe it to them, and Luna too, to try.

"That sounds great, Mom. Maybe we could get some ice cream too?"

Trying. I'm trying.

Dad smiles and ruffles my hair, which he knows I hate but I have a feeling he'll be doing it for years to come. "I'm down for ice cream and I need a new pair of work shoes, so the mall isn't a bad idea."

"Tomorrow? Or do you have plans? Is Sunday better?" She fires questions at me.

"Whenever is fine."

"Tomorrow, then."

They both look at me with smiles and I force one back.

I don't tell them that tomorrow never comes. It's yesterday and today, that's all we ever really have.

CHAPTER TEN

The mall is large and nice, with the kinds of stores I would normally be more than eager to shop in. Today, they look like empty promises full of false happiness.

"What do you think of this?"

I turn around and find my mom holding up a floral dress.

I wrinkle my nose. "It's not really my style."

Her face falls and she looks from the dress to me. "What do you mean? You used to would have loved this."

I shrug. "I don't know. It just looks like a bit much."

She looks at the dress again and puts it back. "I guess you're right. It is pretty bright and the pattern has a lot going on."

I move through the store, letting my fingers skim the fabric of items I pass.

I pluck a few t-shirts, a sweater, and a pair of jeans with patches off racks and counters. "I'm going to go try this stuff on."

My mom looks over her shoulder at the clothes I'm holding. "Okay. I'll be looking. Shoot me a text if you want my opinion on anything."

I nod and head to the dressing rooms. I close and lock the door behind me, dumping the items on the bench inside.

I exhale a breath as I stare at the items. It isn't much, hardly anything compared to what I'd normally try on, but it all feels so needless now.

Anxiety punches a hole in my chest and I feel the rush of sadness hit me out of nowhere.

I feel sad a lot about Luna, about my inability to be the best sister possible to her, that I couldn't fucking save her.

But then there are moments like these where the emotions hit me so deeply, ripping into my chest, that I feel like it's going to smother me.

I back into the mirror, clutching my chest.

My breaths leave me in short inhales and sharp exhales, the air hissing between my lips.

Tears burn my eyes as I sink to the floor, wrapping my arms around my legs. My lips tremble as I sob and memories assault my mind.

"Where are you going?" Luna asks, sitting on the edge of my unmade bed.

"Beck is picking me up and we're going to the lake."

Her face brightens in the reflection of the mirror where I gaze, fiddling with my bikini top and making sure my necklace lays just right.

"Can I come?" She bounces where she sits.

I turn around with a frown, shaking my head. "Sorry, Luna. It's a high school thing."

"Oh." Her face falls. "I don't belong. I'm sorry."

I bend down, searching for my flip-flops on the floor. "I'll take you next weekend. Just me and you. What do you think?"

She worries her bottom lip between her teeth. "Forget about it. I-I have homework to do."

I can sense her shutting down, retreating into herself. "You know I love you, Moon. If I could bring you, I would, but there will be beer and God knows what else. It's not going to be what you're expecting."

Luna's young and her development even younger than her age. The last thing I want to do is expose her to teens doing drugs, drinking, and having sex in parked cars. Someone might take advantage of her and I don't want to have to babysit her all night.

"I know." She exhales a sigh, twisting her hands together—a sure sign she's feeling uncomfortable.

"I love you." I kiss the top of her head. "I have to go." I pause in my doorway and look back at her. "Next weekend, I promise. Just us."

She looks down at her worn sneakers skimming the floor and nods, not looking at me. The sight of her breaks my heart and I walk over to her, bending down on my knees and forcing her to look at me.

"Hey, whatever happens you know I have your back, always, right?"

She twists her lips together, her eyes shifting. "Y-Yeah."

"Good." I smile and pat her knee before standing.

I make it to the hallway before she whispers my name. "Violet?"

"Yeah?" I peek inside at her, her sad eyes meet mine, slightly crossed. I wonder for a moment if I should cancel my plans, but just then my phone vibrates with a text from Beck letting me know she's here.

"Whatever happens, you'll always love me, right?"

"Always, Lu-Lu-Bug."

I snap back to reality, my face wet with tears.

You'll always love me, right?

She knew what she was going to do and I was too dumb to see it. I'm sure she'd decided before then. I don't think for a minute her decision came because I didn't take her with me. No, I think Luna, like with everything in her life, rolled the dice to see where it landed.

If I had said yes and taken her with me, she wouldn't have done it, maybe at all, or maybe just not that day, but I said no and sealed her fate.

I would give anything to go back to that day, to stay home with her, but I didn't and now I'm stuck with that choice.

"Violet?" I hear my mom call into the dressing room.

I scurry to my feet, drying my face with the backs of my hands. Thank God I don't wear makeup like I used to or else my entire face would be streaked with mascara.

"I-I'm here." My voice is thick with tears as I unlock the dressing room door.

Her eyes land on me and her face falls. "Oh, Vi."

"Mommy," I cry out, and dive into her arms. I don't even remember the last time I called her that but in this moment I need my *mommy* not my *mom*.

She wraps me in her arms, rocking me back and forth. "I know, sweetie. I know." She sniffles, exhaling a shaky breath. After a minute she pulls away, but only slightly, and takes my face in her hands. "I know your father and I haven't done the best talking to you about ... about your sister, but *honey*, you can come to us anytime. We're grieving too and we shouldn't shut each other out."

She hugs me against her once more and I clutch her fabric in my fists, never wanting to let go.

"Will this ever get any easier?"

She shakes her head against me. "No, I wish it would. The pain will always be there, but one day, maybe, I hope at least, it won't be as bad. But we'll always miss her. Luna was the light we needed and now that she's gone..."

"We're fumbling through the darkness," I finish for her.

"Exactly." She smiles sadly, letting me go. "Let's find your dad and go home."

We hold each other as we walk out, leaving the clothes behind in the dressing room. After all, they're not what matters, it's the people by your side who do.

CHAPTER ELEVEN

The monotony of school is already wearing on me and it's only been a month. This doesn't bode well for the rest of the school year.

"I'm really starting to think you like me."

I fight a smile as I look up from *Beowulf*—our latest reading assignment—and find Mr. Rochester looking back at me from his desk.

"Seriously, you deserve a better friend than a washed up fifty-something English teacher. Wouldn't you rather socialize with kids your age in the morning instead of me?"

"Aw, don't diss yourself Mr. R. You're the coolest."

He scoffs. "And you're full of shit."

"I just want to do my work, graduate, and move on. I don't have time for friends."

And yet I can't stop watching the boy next-door gaze

through his telescope every night or revel in the brief glimpses I get of him through our bedroom windows.

"You might be the most intelligent seventeen-year-old I know."

"Most of them are pretty stupid, so it's not hard to be smarter."

He laughs, a boisterous belly laugh. "Have you considered joining a club?"

I make a face of disgust. "No." I might have considered it briefly before, but since school has started I don't relish the idea of it.

"Really?" He raises a brow. "I think you should."

I snort. "No."

"Even if me, your favorite teacher, is in charge?"

I hesitate, pulling my bottom lip between my teeth. "What is it?"

"Theatre club." Before I can protest he grabs a flyer from his desk and gets up, handing it to me. "First meeting is this Friday. We're doing *Beauty and the Beast* this year. I encourage you to audition, but you can always work building sets, and doing other behind the scenes stuff."

I look over the sheet of paper in my hands. "I'll think about it."

He grins. "I'm thrilled to hear you're going to do it."

"Mr. Rochester I—"

"Friday, three o'clock in the auditorium, *don't* be late. You know I hate tardiness." The bell rings and his smile disappears, in its place is his stoic frown and downturned brows. "The idiots have been unleashed."

"How has your day been?" I ask Finn, sitting down beside him in the grass. I shuck my backpack off and dig out my lunch.

He doesn't answer, merely giving me a raised brow. Even though it's been a month I don't think Finn completely trusts me yet. That's fine. It'll be all the more worth it once he does.

"I don't know about you, but I'm already dying to go home. Calculus wears me out."

His brows furrow in confusion. "Why? It's easy."

I look at him in surprise. "Then you should be my tutor, because I suck at it."

He shrugs, picking up his ham sandwich. I don't know whether the shrug is meant to be a yes, no, or maybe. But it's progress, so I'll take it.

I rest my back against the brick exterior and take a bite of apple. The sun is bright, but already the trees are starting to change colors. Soon, fall will be here and with it cold weather. I'm not used to the cold and I'm definitely not looking forward to it.

"What's your favorite subject?" I ask him, not expecting an answer.

"Astronomy."

"I didn't know that was taught here." I look at him in confusion.

"It's not." He picks a blade of grass, twirling it between his fingers.

"Oh ... um..."

"I take it at the community college. I ... I like the stars ... space. Planets. All of it. There's more to the world than this." He swings his hand, encompassing the green grass, thick trees, and blue skies.

"I like stars too," I admit quietly. "They remind me of my sister."

"You don't have a sister."

I smile briefly at his bluntness. Finn observes the world and reacts. He doesn't think about tactfulness.

"Not anymore," I sigh, glancing up at the sky.

Finn looks down at his knees, then slowly swings his gaze to me. "I'm sorry?" It comes out as a question, like he's not sure it's the right response.

"Thanks." I tuck a piece of hair behind my ear.

I startle when Finn's fingers touch my cheek. It's the softest graze, but I feel it all the way down to my toes. His blue eyes hold mine for a solid five seconds. I think it's the longest we've ever made eye contact.

"You love her still."

"I'll always love her."

"Hmm," he muses, sitting back and his fingers fall from my cheek. "Love is weird."

"Love is magical," I counter with a soft laugh.

His lips downturn and he tilts his face to the sky. "I wouldn't know."

"Surely, you love your parents?"

He shakes his head. "My dad left when I was little and my mom..." He exhales a heavy breath. "She wants to fix me. Everyone wants to fix me."

"I don't want to fix you."

"Why?"

"Because," I study his profile, his floppy dark hair and glasses, sharp nose, and full lips, "you're you, and that's beautiful. Besides, fixing something implies it's broken. You're not broken."

Just then, the bell rings and we're forced to clean up and head in separate directions for our free period.

But I can't stop thinking about the look on his face when I said who he is, is beautiful. He was surprised, full of wonder, and it makes me sad that he can't see that his differences only make him unique.

CHAPTER TWELVE

"Am I really going to do this?" I mutter to myself, pacing the halls as students leave for the day.

It's not too late for me to go outside, hop on my bike, and leave.

There's no reason for me to actually be considering this. My mom was right, if I'm not going to cheer, why would I do this?

"Ah, Ms. Page. I knew you'd come to your senses and decide to join us. The auditorium is this way."

I jump at Mr. Rochester's voice and he pauses, cocking his head to the side. "You weren't planning to just stand in the hallway all afternoon, right? People might think you're crazy."

"Uh..."

"Good. Follow me."

With no choice but to follow my insane English teacher I end up in the auditorium. Students are already gathered, more than I expected—at least thirty—and I search for a seat.

My eyes stop when I notice Finn sitting on an aisle seat with Jack lying on the floor beside him. As if he senses me he looks up and then away, but I'm even more surprised when he moves his backpack out of the seat beside him and then nods his head to it, offering me to join him.

My heart swells as I move down the aisle and take a seat beside him.

"Thanks," I whisper.

"Welcome." He presses a finger to his lips, looking at the stage stoically but I swear a muscle in his cheek twitches like he's trying not to smile.

Mr. Rochester hops up on stage, letting his legs dangle over the edge.

"Welcome, peasants." He claps his hands. "Some of you are returning and some of you are new." He nods at me. "But you're here nonetheless. Theatre club is more than just a pastime. We're family." Some of the kids clap. "This year's production will be *Beauty and the Beast*. We have a lot of work to do to prepare before spring this year. There's casting, prop building, costumes, and makeup. I hope you all are ready, I only expect the best, and if you half-ass it you're out." He points to the exit. "Most importantly, I do this for fun. Don't fucking ruin it for me, okay, dumbasses?"

We all nod.

"I'm going to pass out the script and I want you guys to partner up and run lines."

I raise my hand. "*Yes*, Ms. Page?"

"What if we don't want to try out?"

"Did I say anything about trying out? I said to partner up and read it. So do it."

I bite my lip, suppressing a laugh. "Yes, sir."

He stares at us a moment longer. "What are you waiting for? A fucking parade? Get to it." He claps loudly.

"Uh ... sir," a guy up front voices, "you didn't give us the script."

"Oh, fuck. Right." He grabs a stack of papers beside him and passes them out.

Once Finn and I each have a script I turn in my seat to face him. "Partners?"

"Sure."

I start out as Belle and he takes the role of Gaston, while we alternate the secondary characters.

"You're really good at this," I remark. Finn becomes a whole new person as he recites the lines. He's completely into it, and no pun intended, theatrical.

He gives me a small, sheepish smile. "My mom forced me to join—she thought I needed to socialize more. I found I actually like it—but don't tell her that," he jokes. "Why are you here? Do you like theatre?"

"Mr. Rochester wanted me to join, so here I am."

"He tends to get what he wants." Finn flips to the next page of the script, reading it over.

"Do you work behind the scenes or will you try for a part?"

"I usually have a small role. Mr. Rochester knows I don't like attention, so I'm usually just a background cast."

"Hmm," I hum.

"What?" He pushes his glasses up where they've slipped down.

"Maybe you should."

"Should what?"

I crack a smile. "Try for a bigger part."

He actually mulls over my words. "I might. I don't have anything to lose. Not anymore."

"What do you mean?"

"In less than a year this place will be nothing but a memory. I can move on with my life. Be anything I want to be, and not what people think I am."

"What do people think you are?" I probe, wanting insight into his mind.

Finn acts like the stares and whispers don't bother him, but clearly they do.

"They call me a freak. A monster. Like I'm less than human, less than them."

My heart fractures inside my chest. "You're more than they'll ever be."

"Sometimes I think they're right." He exhales a heavy sigh.

"They're not."

He looks at me doubtfully. "It's your turn, Belle."

"Right." I duck my head to the script and begin reciting my lines since it's clear he wants to change the subject.

After an hour Mr. Rochester dismisses us with orders to return the following Friday.

"There are only a few weeks where we only meet once a week. Then it moves to several times a week," Finn explains, pushing the doors open to the outside.

"I guess it's a good thing I don't have anything else to do," I joke, but Finn looks hurt. "I was joking, Finn. I actually liked it. I *want* to come back."

"Oh, okay."

"I'll see you," I tell him as we head our separate ways.

I hop on my bike and ride home. The breeze lifts my hair around my shoulders and I soak in the warmth, knowing in a few short weeks it'll be gone. I take the long way home and grab a smoothie, passing by the bookstore as I do. I haven't been back since the first time, and even though I want to return I haven't. It felt like a sign then, like Luna was guiding me, and I'm scared if I go back I won't have that same feeling.

It's silly and makes absolutely no sense, but I want to hold on to the belief for a little longer that Luna was with me in that moment.

I arrive home and my dad's car is already in the driveway. I pale, realizing I didn't tell them I'd be staying late. Since I hadn't made up my mind if I was going to do it or not I didn't bother saying anything, and then when Mr. Rochester spotted me and I ended up in the auditorium I never thought to text my mom.

I'm the fucking worst.

I open the garage and wheel my bike inside, grabbing my smoothie.

The door swings open before my feet touch the stairs leading into the house.

"Violet! Where have you been? I've been worried sick!" My mom admonishes, a hand to her chest. She looks visibly upset and I feel even worse than I did a moment ago.

"I'm so sorry." I inject as much emotion as I can into those three words so she knows I mean it. "I stayed after school, my English teacher suggested I join theatre club so that's where I was, and then I picked up a smoothie when I left."

She exhales a heavy breath. "You scared me. I thought something bad happened and I called the school, but the office people were already gone, I didn't know who else to call, and—"

I cut off her tirade with a hug. "I'm truly sorry, Mom. I didn't mean to worry you. Forgive me?"

I pull away and give her puppy dog eyes and a pout, which has its intended purpose in making her laugh.

"Stop that. I'm mad at you."

"I know, but I really am sorry. I just got caught up and didn't think to text you. I hadn't planned to stay or I would've let you know this morning."

She lets out a weighted breath. "I understand, but that doesn't take away my hours of worry."

Guilt settles in my stomach as we head toward the kitchen and I drop my backpack to the floor.

"I just ... didn't think."

Before Luna, this wouldn't have been an issue, but now my mom is overly worried and paranoid. I don't blame her for it either. She lost a daughter, that's not something she's going to recover from easily.

"We'll be meeting every Friday for the next few weeks, and then it'll be a few times a week. I'm not sure the days yet, but I promise to let you know." I take a sip of my smoothie and she eyes me skeptically. "Where's Dad?" I ask, looking around.

"Walking the neighborhood on foot. We thought you could be in a ditch."

I wince, because she's being serious and not at all joking with me.

"I need to call him," she mumbles to herself, looking for her phone.

I slide it across the counter to her and she calls him.

"Babe, she's here. She just walked in the door. Mhmm. I know. I know. But I was worried. Okay. Love you, too."

She hangs up and looks at me. "I want to ground you, but I'm glad you've decided to join a club, so ... just please let me know when you're staying late or going out. I *can't*..." Her voice cracks. "I can't lose another child. I won't survive it."

"Mom." My tone is guilt-riddled and I stand, wrapping my arms around her. She cries into my shoulder.

"It's the worst kind of loss imaginable." She tightens her hold on me, like if she squeezes me tight enough she'll never have to let me go.

"I'm here. I'm not going anywhere."

"You can't promise that." She pulls away and grabs a tissue from the box on the counter and dries her face.

She turns away, and I exhale a breath, because she's right. I can't make a promise like that. Nothing is guaranteed in this world.

CHAPTER THIRTEEN

After dinner I slip up to my room and shower, changing into a pair of cotton pajama shorts and a tank top. I gather my damp hair on top of my head in a messy bun and brush my teeth. Padding into my room I pull Will Ferret out of his cage and cuddle him in my arms. He lets out happy little noises and I smile, kissing the top of his head.

"You're a good boy." He looks up at me and I scratch under his chin. Luna loved Will. Sometimes, I swear he misses her.

I let him down on the floor to play and spread my books across my bed. I got most of my homework done at school this week, but I still have a few things to finish up. I grab my computer off my desk and sit down on my bed, getting to work. I play music softly from my laptop for background noise. Some people need complete silence to work, but I'm not one of them.

I open up the document I've been working on and try to finish my essay. I only need another page on it, but my brain gave out earlier and I couldn't seem to finish it when I had the chance.

This time, things go smoother and in no time it's done. I submit it through the online portal and breathe a sigh of relief that it's one less thing I'll have to do next week.

There's definitely no way I could've survived this kind of workload and cheered at the same time, but I don't regret choosing to take dual credit classes this year. Cheer was my life for way too long and there are more important things.

Not that cheerleading is bad, or all the girls are snobs, because that's not true. It's a hard ass sport and you build a family with your team, but it became more important to me than my family or school.

But it was also the middle school cheer team who bullied my sister incessantly, all because she had the "audacity" to try out in the first place.

Luna bursts into my room, tears pouring from her eyes. My mouth parts and my phone slips from my hand to my bed. I don't think I've ever seen my sister cry like this before, like her whole soul is shattered.

"Lun—"

I can't even get the question out when she dives onto my bed and wraps her arms around my middle.

"What is it, Lu-Lu-Bug?" I stroke her hair, the same shade of brown as mine.

She sniffles, rubbing her wet face against my chest. "They laughed at me."

"Who laughed at you?" I tug her away, which is difficult considering the sloth hug she has me in.

"The girls," she wipes her snotty nose, "the popular ones."

"What did they laugh at you about?" I probe, wanting to get to the bottom of it.

Anger simmers inside me, at those vicious kids who don't understand my autistic sister and how beautiful, special, and unique she is. But I hide that emotion, because if Luna sees it she'll think I'm angry at her.

"B-Because..." She hangs her head in shame and it breaks my heart. She has nothing to be ashamed of.

"Because? You can tell me anything."

"I-I know, but I shouldn't have done it in the first place." Her crooked teeth dig into her bottom lip.

"Done what?" My brows furrow in puzzlement. I can't imagine Luna doing anything she shouldn't have. She's too shy, too wary of strangers.

"I-I," she stutters and hiccups, more tears brimming her eyes. "I tried out for t-the cheer t-team. I-I wanted to be like you. But they laughed, Violet. They called me dumb. I'm not d-dumb am I?"

My heart shatters for my little sister. She just wants to be like everyone else, but all those kids can see is her autism, as if it somehow makes her less than them or that she carries *some flesh-eating disease they'll catch if they come too close. Growing up with Luna I didn't even realize she was different for a long time. She was only my sister, she still is. I don't see her autism, I see her.*

I grab her shoulders in my hands, and she doesn't want to meet my eyes. I know she's afraid I'll scold her just like they did.

"You did a very brave thing trying out and I'm so proud of you for that. Don't let mean girls like that ever stop you from pursuing your goals. They're mean, catty, and don't deserve someone like you. You shine brighter than all of them."

"I just wanted to be like you, Vi."

I hug her close against my chest, resting my chin on top of her head. "Moon, the only person you need to be in this world is you. Your uniqueness is a gift to the world, not a burden."

Shouting breaks me from the memory and it takes me a moment to reorient myself. At first I think my parents are arguing, but I quickly realizes it's too muffled to be them—besides, even after Luna passed they never argued, not like this. Some couples fall apart in their grief, but I think it brought my parents closer together. They needed each other more than ever.

The shouting continues and I stack my books on top of each other, leaving my laptop on my bed as I get up to investigate. I look out the window beside my bed and see Finn in his room. He's having a complete meltdown and his mom is crying, trying to hold him, but he won't let her. I can't hear distinct words, but I see him push her away, out of his room and slam the door. He falls to the floor, his back against the door and his hands over his ears. He keeps flinching and it makes me think she might be knocking on the door.

I don't know why he's upset, but clearly something has happened.

Finn rocks back and forth and I touch my fingers to the window.

As if drawn by the movement his eyes look out the window, finding me like a ghost across the street. He looks away quickly, burying his face in his hands, and even though I don't want to, I walk away, giving him privacy.

I try to finish a worksheet for my Government classes, but my brain is useless and can only think about the boy next door. I pack up my school stuff and pile it on my desk to finish tomorrow. I put Will Ferret back in his cage, slipping him a few treats and freshening his water. He squeaks happily in response.

I climb into bed, turning out the lights and roll over.

I doze off for an hour, but like always sleep is short-lived. The clock shows it's after eleven as I slip out of bed and climb onto the roof. I hold my legs against my chest, looking at the stars, searching for the brightest one.

When I find it, it sparkles like it's winking and I feel warmth spread through my body. "Hi, Luna."

The night air is getting chilly and when Goosebumps dot my skin I start to climb back inside, but movement catches my eye. Finn marches out the backdoor, but instead of going to his giant round telescope he jogs down the deck steps out to the meadow beyond. He looks angry, or maybe just upset, I can't quite put my finger on it.

I watch until he's a fair distance away and then I hear him scream.

It's a scream of frustration and desperation. Of pain and heartache.

He drops to the grass, his shoulders sagging in defeat. He breathes heavily before lying back in the tall grass, his body all but disappearing.

I climb inside and lock my window. I debate for all of two seconds before I grab a sweatshirt and slip it on. I snag a pair of flip-flops and carry them in my hand as I sneak down the hall, past my parents bedroom, and down the stairs.

Out the backdoor I go, hoping the beep of the alarm isn't loud enough to wake them.

I finally put my shoes on and head through the yard and to the window.

"Finn?" I call softly. It's harder now that I don't have an eagle-eye view to see where he is.

Grass stirs and his dark head pops up. "Violet?"

I hurry over to him and sit down. Unlike at school when we share lunch, there isn't much space between us.

"Are you okay?" I ask him. "You were upset earlier and I saw you leave your—"

"Why do you care?"

I blink at him, taken off guard. "Uh ... I don't know what you mean."

He collapses back into the grass, looking up at the

starry sky. The moon is low and full. After a moment, when he doesn't answer, I lay down beside him.

"You should stay away from me," he says after a while, his voice a soft murmur. He sounds beaten down.

"Why?" I turn my head toward him.

He does the same. "I'm no good for you. For anyone. Look how I treat my mom," he exhales a humorless laugh, "I'm the worst kind of guy around."

"No, you're not."

He swallows thickly, his Adam's apple bobbing. Behind his glasses his eyes are the same color as the sky above us.

"I'm autistic," he whispers like a broken confession.

I hesitate and reach out, brushing my fingers against his cheek. It's smooth, but there's the barest hint of stubble forming. He closes his eyes at my touch and I swear his lips twitch into a smile for a second.

"I know, Finn."

His eyes open in surprise. "You do?"

I nod. I'm sure most of the kids at school know he is. They use it as an opportunity to judge him, to stay away, to not even bother to get to know him or try to include him in anything. People are scared of differences, but they forget none of us are the same.

"You've never said anything," he accuses.

"Why would I?" I skim my fingers over his chin. "You're still you."

"Most people don't like me."

"They don't know you."

"You don't know me," another accusation.

"I want to—when you'll let me."

"Why? I-I don't understand." His dark brows knit together, wrinkling as he tries to puzzle it out.

I let out a soft laugh. "I just do. You remind me of my sister," I admit. "She was autistic."

"Oh." His face falls and he pulls away, my hand falling to the ground between us.

"What?" I ask as his body goes rigid and cold.

"That's why you talk to me. I remind you of her because I'm autistic."

I shake my head. "Finn, that's not why you remind me of her. There's just something about you, this aura, she had the same thing. Sometimes I thought I was the only one who could see it, maybe I am. But..." I bite my lip and his eyes reluctantly return to me. "I never saw her autism. I saw *her*, just like I see *you*. I'm sorry no one else does."

"Some people are nice to me," he muses, rubbing his lips together as his eyes drift back to the sky. "But..."

"They're not your friends," I finish for him.

"I've never had friends before."

His confession breaks my heart.

"I'm your friend."

He rolls his head to the side, his eyes drifting over my features. I wonder what he's thinking. "Okay."

"Okay?" I grin at him.

"You're my friend so I'll be your friend too."

I let out a soft laugh. "Thanks, Finn."

"You're welcome."

He takes everything literally, not catching onto my sarcasm at his casual decision to be my friend. For him, it's not based on a feeling, it's just something he chooses to do. But I hope, one day, he *will* feel something. I want him to know what it's like to have a real friend, someone he can trust and confide in.

"Why were you fighting with your mom?"

He scowls and looks away. His fingers twitch at his side and he sits up, running his hand through his unruly black hair. He lifts one leg up, resting his foot on the ground and his arm on his knee as he looks at the trees. I sit up and I itch to touch him again, but I don't want to push him too much too fast. My question already seems to be causing him distress.

"She wants to fix me," he finally murmurs.

He rips a wildflower from the grass before tearing it into pieces.

"Fix you? What do you mean?"

He wets his lips. "She's always trying to get me to eat these weird foods, or try this new pill, or see a therapist or something. I don't want to do those things."

"You don't have to." His chin dips as he angles his head toward me. "But she *is* your mom. Maybe she's not trying to fix you, just help you, and she doesn't understand you don't want that kind of help."

He shakes his head back and forth, then exhales a heavy, weighted sigh.

Tilting his head, he gazes at the stars. "One day, I'm going to touch the stars, leave this whole place behind. The whole universe is out there and I'm going to float away in it."

Most people might dream of visiting Paris, or Greece, or any number of other places.

But not Finn.

He wants to get lost in the stars.

And me?

I think I want to get lost in him.

CHAPTER FOURTEEN

Exhaling a heavy breath, I raise my fist and knock on the door.

I wait a moment before knocking again. It swings open and I get my first real look at Finn's mom. She's short, he definitely inherited his height from his dad, with the same dark hair he has and blue eyes.

She looks confused seeing me, and offended I'm knocking on her door.

This is off to a great start.

"Hi, can I help you?"

She sounds like she wants to take my order at a drive-thru.

"Um ... hi. I'm Violet. From next door." I point. "I wanted to see Finn."

She looks taken aback. "You're here for Finn?"

My eyes shift around awkwardly. I can't tell if she's pissed, confused, or happy.

"Yeah—I thought he might want to go get coffee. Or … something."

I've never sounded so inarticulate in my entire seventeen years.

A huge smile breaks across her face. "That's wonderful, come in, come in." She ushers me inside with the swish of her hand. She looks ready to pull me into a hug and spin me around. "Finnley's room is upstairs, second door on the right."

"Thanks." I give her a small, awkward wave and take the stairs slowly, feeling her eyes on me as I do.

I reach the door she told me is his, but even if she hadn't I would know. There are stickers of stars, planets, the moon, and rocket ships stuck to it.

I knock softly and there's no reply.

"Finn?" I ask hesitantly.

"Violet?" he blurts, his surprise blatant.

A moment later the door swings open revealing him on the threshold in a pair of tan pants and a gray t-shirt. It's tighter fitting than what he normally wears, the sleeves hugging his shoulders and upper arms.

"Hi." I stand in front of him, my hands clasped together. Now that I'm here I feel silly and unsure of myself.

Behind Finn I spot Jack laying on the floor sans vest, a toy shaped like a banana at his side.

"You're in my house."

I crack a smile at Finn's uncanny ability at stating the obvious.

"I am." I take a breath, getting to the point of why I showed up here. "I thought we could go get coffee? Or go to the bookstore? Lunch, maybe? Or take Jack to the park?" I ramble nervously.

"Why?" He blinks at me behind his glasses, truly puzzled.

"Because, we're friends and that's what friends do." I tuck a piece of hair behind my ear. I've never been this girl before, unsure of herself and shy around a guy. But Finn unbalances my foundation and I find myself wanting him to like me as much as I like him, but it's impossible to know where I stand with him. "We're friends, right?"

I hope he's remembering last night as vividly as I am.

The moments I'm with Finn, it's like time pauses and everything becomes super-focused and I'm hyper aware of the smallest details, but maybe for him it's not that special.

"Oh, I guess you're right." He tilts his head, either appraising me or contemplating something. After a moment he says, "I like coffee and books are nice."

I grin, resisting the urge to clap my hands. "Can you go now?"

He rubs his lips together and nods, his dark hair flopping. He pushes it out of his eyes. "I-I can drive us."

"Cool. Let me run home and tell my parents we're going."

He nods, his attention already gone from me as he whistles at Jack.

I leave him and my feet pound down the stairs. The smile I wear seems to be permanently plastered to my face.

"How'd it go?"

A scream erupts from my throat before my hand can reach for the front door knob. His mom has her head poked around the corner where I assume the kitchen is.

Placing a hand against my racing heart I turn to face her. "Good, we're going to get coffee and browse the bookstore."

Her whole face lights up and she clasps her hands. "Oh, that's excellent."

The fact that something so simple as her son going out for a few hours with a friend brings her so much joy tells me how this has probably never happened before and it breaks her heart how her son isn't included in normal things like he deserves to be.

"I have to run home and let my parents know I'm leaving." I toss a thumb over my shoulder.

"Oh, oh, of course." She waves me on. Before I can close the door behind me I hear her say, "Thank you."

I don't reply, because she doesn't have to thank me for being her son's friend.

I just am.

———

AFTER FACING the Spanish Inquisition and getting more questions about Finn than necessary, I'm free to go.

I run outside and over to Finn's car, an old Honda Element in an olive green color.

The windows are rolled down and Jack sits on the passenger seat.

"No, Jack. I said in the back. You have to move." Finn argues with the dog, trying to force him into the back. The dog is stubborn and persistent, Finn is barely able to budge him, and I'm sure the dog is used to being beside him and feels like he'd be doing something wrong to get in the back.

"It's fine, Finn. I can sit in the back."

"No!" He cries, his blue eyes shooting to mine across the seats. "I-I want you to sit here." He looks away, like he's scared I'll be mad or disgusted by his statement.

"Okay," I say slowly. "Then I'll help."

I open the door to help him move Jack to the back when the dog jumps into the back on his own.

Finn turns around and glares at his dog, who I swear is smiling the way his tongue lolls out of his mouth.

"You did that on purpose," Finn grumbles. He exhales a breath and his eyes slide to me as I sit down and close the door. "Buckle your seatbelt. Around five-thousand people a year die from not wearing a seatbelt. Don't be a statistic."

I stifle my laughter, pulling the seatbelt across my body. I was already going to buckle up, but Finn's knowledge and worry is adorable.

Once my seatbelt clicks in place he checks all the mirrors and makes sure everything is as it should be. Hand hovering over the gearshift he looks at me. "This is weird."

"Getting coffee?"

"Having someone in my car."

I soften. I itch to squeeze his hand but I refrain. "I can take my bike and meet you there."

He shakes his head. "No. That's silly."

He exhales a long, deep breath and puts the car in reverse.

I try to ignore the fact his mom is watching out the window just like my parents are.

The fall air stirs my hair as we drive into town, and I feel more relaxed than I have in months. For the moment, at least, my thoughts are quiet and peaceful. I don't feel at war within myself. Finn keeps his eyes steadily on the road, and the more minutes that pass the calmer he becomes. The tension leaves his grip on the wheel first, then his shoulders.

We reach the quaint town center and he pulls into a spot in front of the shops. He turns the key, shutting off the ignition and sits with his palms flat on his legs, staring ahead.

I stay quiet, picking at the tear in the knee of my jeans. Jack sits up in the back, poking his head between the seats. He rubs his head against Finn's arm and Finn finally moves.

"Coffee," he states, almost as if to remind himself that coffee isn't such a big deal. He opens the door and gets out, letting Jack climb through to his seat before securing the leash on him.

I get out and meet him at the back of his car where we wait to cross the street.

We walk side by side, not saying a word. I don't find it uncomfortable. Too many people want to fill the world with meaningless chatter. When you speak, what you say should matter.

The coffee shop is down the street. I've been a few times already and it's one of those cute shops with exposed brick, writing on the walls, and an eclectic style. Music from the eighties and nineties seems to be the only thing on the playlist and it has a relaxed vibe.

I hold the door open and let Finn go in first since he's holding Jack.

He hesitates, eyeing the long line.

I pause beside him, assessing his body language—the nervous way he swallows, and how his eyes dart around every corner as if looking for an attack.

I hook my pinky through his and he looks down at our joined fingers then up at me. I open my mouth to ask him if it's okay, but he smiles and I have my answer.

We get in line and I look at the menu, deciding what I want. As we get closer Finn's fingers fiddle with Jack's leash and his breaths are uneven.

"Do you know what you want?" I'm hoping if I can get his mind off things he'll be less bothered.

I know with my sister it was the *thought* of certain things that was far more upsetting than actually enduring them.

He rubs his left ear against his shoulder and then does the same with his right one. "Loud. It's loud in here."

My mouth parts and I realize that just like that first day in Physics, noise is one of his triggers, and he's right it *is* loud in here. I didn't notice since it doesn't bother me, and because of that fact I didn't consider how he might feel in here.

"Tell me what you want and I'll get our drinks, we can sit outside."

I point to the scattered tables out front where there are far less people. The traffic isn't loud or crazy since this is a small town so I hope he'll be fine there waiting for me.

"Okay." His jaw clenches and unclenches as he eyes the menu. "S'mores mocha. A medium."

I give him a small smile and unhook our fingers. "You got it. Anything else? A snack?"

"Chocolate croissant."

"That's my favorite too."

His eyes lighten like he's pleased by this fact. "Really?"

"Yep. We have more in common than you think." I bump his shoulder with mine. "Now go on, I'll be fine here and I'll meet you outside."

He nods, his eyes darting over my face, taking in my pink cheeks and glossy lips, the hair falling over my forehead and every little freckle and detail in between.

He turns to leave and then stops. "Thank you," he whispers.

Before I can respond his long stride is taking him outside.

I smile to myself, lifting my hands to my cheeks that I know have to be bright red now.

The line moves forward and I place our order, handing over the cash and getting my change before I stand to the side to wait for it to be ready.

It doesn't take long and I carry the two steaming hot beverages outside along with the bag containing the croissants.

Finn sits at the table, tapping his fingers on the tile top. Jack lays at his feet, his leash not attached to anything. The dog is trained to not leave Finn's side, but I think even if he wasn't he'd still choose to stay there.

I set everything down and plop in the chair beside him.

"What did you get?" He points to my steaming cup.

"Chai tea latte." I pass him the dessert—at least I consider it a dessert—and grab my own.

"Chai tea latte," he repeats, as if committing it to memory. He taps a beat with his fingers on his leg before leaning forward and tearing a piece of the croissant off and taking a bite.

I do the same to mine, stifling a moan as the warm chocolate melts on my tongue.

A soft wind stirs the leaves on the trees lining the street, the sun above bathing us in a much-needed warmth.

Finn's long fingers wrap around his cup and he takes a sip. He looks around, taking in everything on the street, from the passing cars to the people strolling by. He looks more at ease than he does at school, but still not quite comfortable. I wish I could ease his worries, but he also has every right to feel those emotions.

I sip my latte and finish the rest of my croissant. Finn only eats half of his and I wrap it up in a napkin, laying it inside the paper bag. He watches my movements, head bowed.

"Should we go to the bookstore? Or we can go home?" I want to give him the option, because if he's feeling strung out I don't want to force him to do even more socializing.

There are so many varying types of autism. It isn't one

size fits all. The quirks my sister had aren't going to be the same for Finn.

He stands, picking up Jack's leash and grabbing his coffee in the other. "I want to go to the bookstore. There's something I'm looking for."

I smile, pleased that our outing isn't over yet. Being with Finn reminds me I'm not alone.

I join him around the table and we walk down the street side by side.

"How long have you lived here?" I smile as a little kid chases after bubbles in the park across the street.

"All my life." His gaze flicks down to me, squinting from the brightness of the sun. "Why'd you move here?"

"My dad was offered a transfer. He works in IT for a bank. But..." I pause, my steps stilling.

Finn walks a few more paces before he realizes I'm not beside him and turns around.

"But what?"

"I think they just wanted to get away, from the reminders of my sister. It was hard, seeing her everywhere but knowing she's gone."

"Is she buried there?"

His question surprises me for some reason, but I guess it makes sense.

I shake my head as we start walking again. "She was cremated. We scattered her ashes."

His lips twitch in thought. "Are you afraid you'll forget her?"

"I'm afraid of forgetting the sound of her voice, or her laugh, little things like that. But no, I'm not scared of forgetting *her*. That would never be possible. She'll always be here." I touch my fingers to my heart, coming to a stop as we wait for the crosswalk.

"What's the animal I see you with sometimes?"

Looking straight ahead, I smile. Even though I try not to peek across at Finn's room too often it makes me feel better to know he *does* look back sometimes.

"I have a ferret."

"A ferret?" He blurts as the sign changes and we cross the street. "Why would you have a ferret of all things?"

I laugh, bumping his shoulder with mine. "Because they're fun and cute. His name is Will Ferret."

His brows narrow. "That's a horrible name for a ferret."

"We'll agree to disagree on that one." I wink and he looks confused for a moment before smiling back.

Reaching the bookstore he grabs the door and this time waits for me to go first.

"Thank you," I whisper, feeling a flush come to my cheeks. It feels like such a silly reaction over a simple gesture, but my body loves to betray my feelings.

The chiming of the door sends the older man, once more behind the counter, looking up from the volume he's reading.

"Ah, back again." He looks behind me, smile brightening. "And you've brought my favorite, most voracious customer with you."

Finn waves. "Hi, Pete. Is my order in?"

Pete closes his book and snaps his fingers. "It is. Let me grab it for you."

He disappears into the back and I turn to Finn, cocking my head to the side. "Come here often?" It's a poor joke, and obviously falls flat.

"I like books." He speaks softly, and from his tone I have a feeling this is yet another thing he's been judged on.

"I don't read often enough," I admit, picking up a hard-back of old fairytales from the display table.

Finn picks up a book and flips through it. "I figure if I never make it to space, at least I'll have traveled the world in my mind, and lived more lives than one."

"That's an interesting way of putting it."

"Ah, here you go." Pete returns and hands Finn the book already in a bag.

"Thanks, Pete. Violet and I are going to look around a bit."

A shiver goes up my spine when he says my name. He doesn't speak it often, and when he does it sends tiny charges zinging through my body.

"Take your time." Pete waves us off, picking up his book once more and sitting down to read.

"What kind of books do you read?" My voice is hushed, like we're in a library, as we move down the aisles.

"Everything."

"Everything?"

He hangs his head. "My mom tells me I need to use better descriptors and one word answers aren't answers at all." He grabs a book from a shelf, looking at the back. "I like non-fiction, anything from history to of course space, I love fantasy, and I even like Anime."

"Anime?" I raise a brow, my voice laced with surprised. "I wasn't expecting that."

"Have you read any?" I shake my head and a slow grin lifts his lips. "This way."

I follow him between the narrow, cluttered aisles and he stops at the last shelf and kneels on the floor. I spot the tiny section of Anime books and he scans the titles before choosing one.

"Read this one."

The cover shows a black and white drawing of a girl and a boy sitting back to back. One of his legs is stretched out, with the other raised, his arm dangling loosely over it. Above them are stars and planets. I recognize Saturn, but none of the others.

"Why this one?"

"Because he's an alien from outer space, and everyone judges them for their relationship, but she loves him anyway."

"Oh." I use the edge of my nail to trace the lines of her face. "I'll get it then."

We peruse the aisles some more and I grab one more book, something that looks like a sweet read, and Finn grabs three more.

"How long does it take you to finish a book?"

He shrugs, Jack panting at his side. "Depends."

I give him a look and he actually lets out a small chuckle.

"If it's long, a day, something short only takes me a few hours if that."

"Wow. I'm impressed. I'm a slow reader." I don't know why it feels like a sucky thing to admit.

"Everyone reads at their own speed."

We check out with our finds and head out. I toss my now empty coffee cup into the trashcan on the street and Finn does the same.

The walk back to his car is silent between us, but it's nice.

Finn opens the back door and Jack hops inside easily.

"Oh, now you don't fight with me," Finn grumbles, ruffling Jack's ears good-naturedly.

I slide into the passenger seat, placing my bag of books between my feet.

"This was nice," I remark, pulling the seatbelt across my body before he can say anything.

He wets his lips and nods. "I..." He pauses, shaking his head. His dark hair flops in his eyes and he shoves it back, glancing over at me. "I had fun." He gives me a small hesitant smile and I answer it with a grin of my own.

The whole drive home, I look out the window with a smile dancing on my lips.

For weeks Finn barely spoke back to me, and now here we are spending hours at a time together.

I wish the kids at school would give him a chance, because they're missing out on having a friendship with an amazing person, but I'm selfishly glad I get him all to myself.

If Luna is the brightest star in the sky, then Finn is the biggest planet, and I've been sucked into his orbit.

CHAPTER FIFTEEN

I'LL NEVER UNDERSTAND WHY PEOPLE THINK STARING is okay.

As I navigate the crowded halls, headed toward the cafeteria, eyes of my fellow classmates follow me.

I hear the whispers.

She's weird.

She's too quiet.

She only talks to that freak.

It's not their words that bother me, it's the fact that this time last year I was one of them. I spoke about people behind my hand, gossiping untruths when I hadn't ever bothered to know the person I was speaking of.

I can't blame them for their ignorance, not when I was exactly like them, but I am frustrated by it. People, not just teens, take things at face value and don't bother to delve further than what they can see.

Ever since my first day when I talked back to that one girl I've set myself apart. I plastered a target on my back for nothing more than daring to go against the social norm.

Why is that?

Why are we so incapable as human beings to sympathize with another?

It's baffling.

The cafeteria is packed, fuller than normal, and when I look outside I see why.

It's pouring down rain, the storm having come out of nowhere. This morning the sun was shining.

My hold tightens on my backpack straps as I look around.

Again, many eyes stare at me. It's not a collective thing, no I'm not worth that, but I can see eyes at several different tables drift to me and away. I swear I hear snickers, but that might only be in my head, an echo of my own long ago malicious laughter.

It's never that I was knowingly mean, just like these kids hardly ever say anything to me, but quiet judgment is just as bad as a sharp tongue.

Sometimes it's even worse because of the assumptions you can make.

I start to turn back down the hall, figuring I'll find a quiet place to eat on my own since there's no chance Finn's outside and I have no idea where he'd go on a nasty day like this, when movement catches my eye.

A grin I can't control sets over my face as I spot Finn, Jack sitting by his feet, trying to flag me down.

My heart lurches and then begins to beat even faster as I take the needed steps to stand in front of him.

"It's raining," he announces.

"I noticed." My hold on my straps loosen.

"Do you still want to eat with me?" He ducks his head, suddenly unsure and maybe a little embarrassed for flagging me down.

"Of course."

His cheeks turn a soft shade of pink and he nods, signaling me to follow him.

I'm surprised when we reach a pair of doors down a corridor I've never been, but I'm pretty sure is beside the auditorium.

Finn holds up a finger to his lips. "No one knows I have this. Our secret, right?"

"Our secret," I echo as he pulls a key out and unlocks the door.

I follow him into the darkened space and find that we're on the stage, behind the thick curtain. He turns a light on and it illuminates the space in a dull glow.

It's not much to eat by, but I don't mind. There's something intimate about it.

Finn's steps make a dull sound across the stage and he sits down beside me, stretching his long legs in front of him.

"If there were stars on the ceiling it'd be kind of like our meadow."

Our.

My heart latches onto that one word, cherishing it infinitely more than I've ever treasured a single word before.

"How do you have a key?"

"Mr. Rochester." He gives a small, casual shrug, digging in his bag for his lunch.

Jack lies down beside him, resting his head on his paws. His brown eyes follow Finn's movements and once he sees Finn's brown paper bag he lets out a satisfied breath. The dog's eyes move to me and I swear he gives me an almost appreciative look, like he's thankful he's not Finn's only companion anymore.

"Why did Mr. Rochester give you a key?"

Finn shrugs, pulling an apple out and taking a bite. He chews, the crunch of the juicy apple seeming too loud in the empty auditorium.

"He knows I like my space. I can come here and ... breathe." He looks at me with questioning eyes, wondering if I understand what he's saying.

I nod, popping a grape into my mouth. "Makes sense."

I look around at all the equipment backstage. Wires, pulleys, and other things I have no idea what they are. I guess since I've joined the theatre club I'm going to grow well acquainted with this place. When I got suckered into joining by Mr. Rochester, I wasn't sure I'd return, but the fact that Finn is a part of it makes it not half-bad. At least I don't have to pretend to socialize with people I don't want to know.

I grab my turkey sandwich from the Ziplock baggie and take a bite. Finn watches my movements like everything I do is absolutely fascinating. He clears his throat and fumbles in his backpack, slipping a treat to Jack.

"Why does Jack have a regular name? Why not a planet or constellation?"

"He came with the name."

I snort, crumbs spraying from my mouth in an embarrassing manner. "That makes it sound like he's a toy."

Finn looks at his dog with quiet interest. "He's my friend."

The special bond between them is obvious. Maybe all service dogs are like that with their person, but I wouldn't know. This is my first experience ever being close to someone who has one.

"I know he is."

Finn gives me a soft smile. In the distance the bell rings and we wad up our trash and dispose of it in a bin. Heading out the way we came Finn locks up before we part ways.

———

THE REST of the day drags by and the storm rages on outside. I rode my bike like always, but there's no way I can take it home like this. I find a seat on one of the benches lining the entrance, getting ready to call my mom and ask if she can get me.

"Violet?"

My head snaps up and I look up at Finn standing in front of me. He adjusts his glasses and looks anywhere but my face.

"I thought you might want a ride home ... since it's raining ... if you don't, it's cool, I wanted to ask."

I smile gratefully. "That would be great. Thank you. Do you think it's possible for me to fit my bike in the back of your car?"

He ponders my question for a moment. "I think it will."

He follows me out and I wave him away. "Go to your car. There's no point in you getting soaking wet too."

"I want to help." The rain beats down on us, and despite his rain jacket and hood—he's definitely more prepared than I am—the ends of his hair are getting wet and water speckles his glasses.

"Okay," I agree.

I unlock my bike from the rack and then we move at a slight jog to his car. Poor Jack only has a vest to keep him dry, but since his tongue is lolling out and he looks happy I don't think he's too bothered by it.

We reach Finn's car, now completely soaked to the bone, and he unlocks it then opens the trunk.

"I'll help you once Jack's in."

I wait while he lets Jack onto the backseat. It only takes a minute, not even, and I'm so chilled from the rain now I'm positive if I remove my shoes my feet will be blue.

Finn jogs back to my side.

"On three," I tell him. "One, two, three."

We lift together, and I nearly drop my end because I get distracted by the movement of his bicep and the long vein running down his forearm. My mouth goes dry and I know I'm staring, but I can't help it. Finn is outrageously attractive and he has no idea what he does to me.

With mostly his help we get my bike inside and the trunk closed.

We hurry into the car and he turns it on, blasting the heat to hopefully knock off the chill.

The icy rain must be trying to remind us all that summer is over and fall is here. The unusually warm weather—for here, at least—has been much appreciated. I'm not sure this Texas girl is ready for a snowy winter. In fact, I've never actually *seen* snow. Not in person, anyway.

I shoot my mom a text, letting her know I'm getting a ride with Finn so she doesn't worry or decide to come get me.

Finn backs out and joins the long procession of cars leaving the school grounds. Between the students, teachers, and buses, it takes thirty minutes to finally leave.

"Thank you for the ride." I slip out of his car into the rain.

"Let me help you with your bike." He fumbles with his seatbelt and joins me. He ends up lifting it out himself and I grab the handlebar, letting the weight of the bike lean against me.

"Thank you again, Finn."

He nods.

I should get out of the rain, we both should, but we don't.

Exhaling a shaky breath I stand on my tiptoes and kiss his cheek, dangerously close to the edge of his lips.

A small gasp leaves him and I hurry away, towing my

bike toward my home and garage, before I can see any sort of expression on his face. I'm mostly afraid I'll see something I don't want to see, like indifference, and I've already had my heart ripped apart from my sister's death.

I don't need a boy to crush the rest of it.

CHAPTER SIXTEEN

Plopping my ass down in the seat beside Finn I let out a disgruntled breath. "All anyone can talk about is homecoming."

His brows lift and he watches me out of the side of his right eye.

Despite his silence I rant on.

"It's homecoming this and homecoming that." My hands gesture wildly around me. "What dress to wear, shoes, hair, makeup. It's all so ... boring." I release a pent up breath. "I think that's why it's bothering me. I used to obsess over school dances and having a date, but now ... well, I still want to go even though I understand there are more important things than a dance. Is that silly?"

He shakes his head. "If you want to go you should."

"You should go with me," I blurt, and realize I've basically asked him to be a date.

Actually, there's no *basically* about it. That's exactly what I've done.

"No." He eyes the stage ahead, avoiding me so I can't see his panicked expression.

"Yeah," my shoulders deflate, "I shouldn't go anyway. I don't really know anyone and dances aren't fun without friends."

"I thought I was your friend?" His head whips up to me, eyes wide.

"You are." I place a gentle hand on his forearm. "But you just said you didn't want to go—ergo I would be alone."

"*Ergo*, Ms. Page, pay attention," Mr. Rochester snaps from his position on the stage.

My cheeks color at being called out.

I force my thoughts away from the school dance and focus on Mr. Rochester's words as he discusses the play and his plans for the upcoming auditions next week.

An hour later we're dismissed to head home and I follow Finn outside.

After the Monday rainstorm he was leaning against his car Tuesday morning, hands shoved into the pockets of his jeans, and gave a single nod toward his car.

I took him up on the offer and we've ridden to and from school together every day since.

Jack sniffs at the grass and hikes up his leg on a bush. Finn and I wait for him to finish his business and continue down the sidewalk.

Leaves swirl around my feet, already turning red and

orange in the late September weather. I toe my sneaker against the ground, kicking a rock out of the way.

Finn unlocks his car and I shuck off my heavy backpack, climbing in and buckling my seatbelt quickly.

Once Jack is situated in the back Finn gets in and a small grin tugs his lips when he sees I'm already buckled.

He starts the car and backs out slowly. He's a good driver, even if at times I think my presence makes him uncomfortable.

We're almost home when he says, "You need to try out."

I snort. "For the play? No." I shake my head adamantly.

His fingers flex against the steering wheel. "I-If you do, then I will too."

I nearly choke on my own tongue. "What?"

He shrugs. "I've done small parts—a line here and there if it's necessary. I've basically filled in for background parts Mr. Rochester needed someone for. But..." He pauses, gathering his breath, while I use every moment to form my argument on why this is a very bad idea for me. "I have nothing to lose."

"Why?" It seems to be the only word I can form.

"It could be the start of something new—the beginning of something great. My mom always tells me not to close a door before I've even opened it. Maybe it's time I start listening to her."

I sit stunned in the passenger seat, Jack's pants become the only thing I can hear other than the blood rushing through my head, when Finn says nothing else.

He pulls into his driveway and kills the engine. Before I can hop out and run away, he undoes his seatbelt and leans toward me. "You make me brave, Violet. I want to make you brave too."

Staring into deep blue eyes I know there's no way I can deny him this request.

"Fine."

He grins triumphantly and his happy smile makes my agreement worth it. After all, theatre already isn't that bad with his company. If we both have a bigger part, it's more time together.

He holds up a pinky and I'm reminded of the day at the coffee shop when I hooked my pinky with his. Clearly, he hasn't forgotten.

I wrap mine around his. "Together." There's uneasiness in his eyes, but a determination as well.

If Finn is willing to put himself out on a limb then I can do it too.

"Together," I echo.

———

Pots banging, jazz music playing, and the scent of spices hit my nose. I toe off my sneakers and drop my backpack by the stairs, padding into the kitchen.

A smile touches my lips, watching my mom dance around the kitchen preparing dinner.

She used to do it all the time before Luna passed away. It's something I thought I might never see again, and her simple happiness brings me joy.

I'm still grieving.

She's still grieving.

But it doesn't mean we're not allowed a few moments to feel normal.

She turns around and jumps when she sees me. "Oh, Vi! I didn't hear you come in."

She reaches over and turns down the volume on the Bluetooth speaker.

"Just got in." I head over to the refrigerator and open it up. My eyes scan the various food items inside—it's always well stocked, my mom hates not having any possible ingredient she might need—and I grab a grape, tossing it into my mouth. It pops when I bite down, the sour juice hitting my tongue. I chew and swallow it, then grab a handful before bumping the door closed with my hip.

"How was your club?"

"Good." I shrug. "What are you making? It smells yummy."

I eye the hodgepodge of ingredients, unable to discern what they could possibly make.

"Fettuccine with red pepper alfredo sauce. I'm adding steak too."

"Never would've guessed that, but it sounds delicious."

I bite into another grape, watching her move about the kitchen. The kitchen is her happy place, where her mind is free of burdens and she can simply exist, but what's mine? I don't know. It used to be my friends, but I understand now depending on other people for my happiness doesn't work. I have to find it within myself.

I like the night, I suppose. The peace and quiet of a

sleeping house, with nothing but the stars and my thoughts to keep me company. Even if they're bad thoughts, I still live for those moments when I slip onto the roof and gaze at the sky.

"Where'd you drift off to?" Mom stirs the sauce in a pan, looking at me over her shoulder.

"Just thinking."

"How ... how are you doing?" Her face is pained and I know she isn't asking in general about my well-being.

"I'm..." I lace my fingers together, laying them on the countertop. "Coping."

I see no other choice in the matter. I'm okay with my grief, most days anyway, it's a reminder of my love for my sister. If I didn't love her with all my heart and soul then I wouldn't feel her loss like the ache of a missing limb. But I *do* have to cope, and I think in some strange way Finn has shown me that.

When she's silent I ask her the same question. "How are *you* doing?"

"Contemplating my entire existence."

Her face crumples and within a second I'm joining her around the counter and pulling her into my arms. She holds me to her, like the tighter she holds me the more grounded she'll feel.

I miss my sister something fierce, but I can't imagine what my parents feel losing a child. I'm not even at the age where I'm thinking about children, but even now, if I do consider my future and kids, the thought of having to bury one of them is more excruciating than I can comprehend. It's the worst kind of torture.

"I love you." She runs her fingers through my dark hair like she used to do when I was a little girl.

"I love you too, Mom." I squeeze her tighter.

"I wish it didn't hurt so much." She lets me go and rubs the backs of her hands under her eyes. Somehow her makeup isn't smudged from her tears.

I tilt my head to the side and shrug. "Pain deserves to be felt. If you don't feel it, then was the love even real?"

She lets out a surprised laugh. "You're far wiser than I was at your age, Vi."

I snort. I'm only wiser because Luna killed herself and I had to grow up and stop being that girl who was a clueless airhead.

"We all have to grow up eventually," I say instead. "I just had to do it sooner than most."

I whisper the last part under my breath as I walk out of the kitchen.

Grabbing my bag, I lug the heavy sack upstairs and drop it in my desk chair. A shower is calling my name so I do just that and change into a jog bra, sweatpants, and one of my old cheer shirts. I thought about getting rid of them, but cheer was a part of me, it always will be, and I don't want to forget the good times or the pride Luna always radiated when she came to see me.

Slipping my feet into a pair of slippers I make my way downstairs, my dad's voice now having joined my mother's. I pause on the bottom stair, eavesdropping on their conversation. I know I shouldn't, but my conscience doesn't stop me.

"You've been crying," my dad's warm voice says softly.

"Only a little."

"I'm sorry, baby. I wish I could make all of this go away."

"I don't. I'd rather feel everything than nothing at all."

I hear him kiss her tenderly, and decide it's time to make my presence known.

"Dad? Are you home?"

He turns away from my mom as I enter the kitchen and flashes me a smile.

"There's my girl."

I finch.

Girl, not *girls*, like it was only a few short months ago.

He notices my reaction and frowns. He has more wrinkles around his mouth than he's ever had before.

"I'm okay."

I won't break.

He clears his throat and wraps his arms around me. "Hungry?"

"I guess so."

I grab a plate and start piling pasta and sauce onto it. It smells delicious, but my stomach is suddenly silent.

We all sit down to eat like we always do. I don't mind the time with my parents, but that doesn't mean it isn't monotonous and boring on occasion.

"How's school?"

I look across at my dad. "Fine."

"What colleges are you thinking about applying to?"

My applications need to go out soon—way too soon—and I haven't been giving it enough thought.

"Not sure yet."

His fork clangs against the bowl, dropping from his surprised fingers. "Violet, it's crunch time. You need to get your applications in order, your admittance essays, I don't know what you're—"

"Anthony." My mom places her hand over his, her eyes sliding to me. "Give Vi a break."

"She doesn't have time for—"

"He's right." I force a smile at my mom. "I need to get that taken care of."

"I can help you," he insists.

I stir the pasta around my bowl. "Thanks, Dad. I might take you up on that."

I doubt I will. Even though I know he'd offer valuable advice, he'll also want me to go to a certain type of school and get a certain type of degree. I don't know what I want, and I won't have it decided for me either. I know it doesn't come from a malevolent place, he truly wants what's best for me, but no one knows that but me. I just have to figure it out.

We finish dinner and I load the dishwasher.

"We're putting a movie on, Vi, you want to join?" My mom calls from the family room.

The dishwasher clicks into place and I start it.

I want nothing more than to escape to my room with Will Ferret, but I also know moments like this are fleeting. In less than a year I'll be off to college, starting my own life, and movie nights with my parents will be no more.

My chest aches with that realization. As much as my parents can bug me—doesn't everyone's—I love them wholly. They always wanted to be close to me and Luna, making time for special family nights. Ones I never missed, even when I was caught up in my own social life.

"Yeah," I call back. "I'll pop some popcorn."

I pull the canteen of kernels from the pantry and fix them in the microwaveable popper with oil. I stick it in the microwave and push the button. I listen carefully to the pops and when they start to slow I pull it out before it can burn and add movie theater butter to it. The stuff is greasy and artery clogging, but it's a popcorn *must*.

Carrying the popcorn with me to the couch, I curl up in the empty spot they left between them for me. I pull the blanket over top my crossed legs and exhale a breath.

Fast and the Furious comes on the screen and I smile at the old family favorite.

By the time the movie ends it's late, and we all trudge our tired butts up to bed.

I ease my bedroom door closed and let Will out for a little bit. He runs in circles and twirls happily when I offer him a treat. When I feel like he's tired out I put him away with promises to take him on a walk tomorrow—yes, I walk my ferret, he deserves fresh air too.

Drawn to the window overlooking the backyard I notice Finn's figure in the distance. As if he senses me he turns and waves. It's not a wave of hello, it's an invitation.

I don't hesitate.

I yank on a sweatshirt and put on some warm boots so I don't freeze to death in the fall night. From what I could see from the window Finn was only in sweatpants and a long sleeve shirt, but while these temperatures feel downright artic to me, I'm sure it's nothing more than a cool breeze to him.

I tiptoe my way down the hall and stairs, slipping outside.

If my parents ever get wind of my late night meadow adventures with Finn they're likely to lock me in my room and throw away the key—the ironic part is I used to sneak out for far more nefarious reasons.

The tall grasses in the meadow brush against my clothed legs, making a rustling noise that is probably no more than a whisper in the night but sounds like thunder to my ears.

I reach the spot where Finn sits, one knee drawn to his chest and his arms draped over it. He quirks his head to the side as I join him, crossing my legs under me.

"You haven't been using your telescope as much," I comment, wiggling my butt around as I try to get comfortable on the hard earth.

He shrugs, rubbing his lips together. I look up at the stars, not expecting an answer from him, so I'm shocked when he does speak.

"I'm learning sometimes the things closest to us are worth seeing too. We see them every day and after a while we stop taking notice, but when you look with a sharper eye you find things you never spotted before."

I turn my head, expecting him to be looking at the night sky, but he's looking at me instead.

I freeze as his hand comes up slowly and his index finger gently touches my cheek. He pulls away and I squint in the darkness, staring at the tip of his finger.

An eyelash.

"Make a wish," he murmurs, his voice deep and almost husky. "I don't believe wishes come true, but that doesn't mean they aren't worth making."

My eyes meet his for a second before he drops them, still not comfortable making eye contact, and I close mine, thinking of a good wish. When I have it my breath falls upon his finger and the eyelash disappears into the night.

"Why don't you believe in wishes?"

He lies down, keeping his one leg bent, and tucks his right arm behind his head. His shirt rides up a bit, exposing a small sliver of his smooth stomach and dark hair beneath his belly button. He turns his head slightly in my direction and it makes me angry how much I want to fit my body into the curve of his left side. Back in Texas I had a few flirtations with different boys, but nothing that ever made me feel like *this*.

Like my heart is going to beat out of my chest.

Like my skin hums with a song only he can create with the barest touch.

Like gravity doesn't exist and I'm floating through outer space.

I lay down, turning on my side to face him, waiting for his response.

"They never come true. I wished for my dad to come back—not for me, but for my mom and brother and sister. But it's not the wish we need. It's the hope."

"You have a brother and sister?" I'm startled by this revelation.

"Yeah, they're in college."

"What are their names?" My curiosity gets the better of me. It's so rare to get any tidbit of personal information from Finn. I don't think it's that he does it on purpose, he just doesn't deem it necessary.

"Husten and Della."

"Husten, Della, and Finnley," I murmur, and a soft shudder of a breath passes through his lips like hearing me say his full name does something to him.

Lying down on my back I spread my arms at my sides and look up at the night sky.

I startle when his pinky hooks into mine but then smile to myself.

We stay like that for a while, twenty minutes at least, before he sits up.

"We should go to bed."

"We should," I echo, following suit.

But I don't want to.

We trek through the grassy meadow and he pauses before we reach the spot where we need to part to head to our respective houses.

He cocks his head to the side, and I can tell thoughts are darting through his mind.

"Goodnight, Nebula. You're my new favorite part of the night."

He takes off for his house, his long steps carrying him away in seconds.

I stand there stunned, but there's no denying the butterflies in my belly.

CHAPTER SEVENTEEN

Nebula.

Nebula.

Nebula, Nebula, Nebula.

The nickname repeats through my head all through the night and into the next morning. I looked up what a nebula was exactly, a giant cloud of dust floating out in space, but what stood out to me the most is some are where new stars form and that sounds pretty cool to me.

Will Ferret scurries through my bedroom as I get ready for the day. It might be the weekend, but I don't plan to vegetate in my pajamas all day.

It's nice out, but according to my phone a little chilly, so I put on a pair of jeans and a sweater. I swipe on a little mascara and gloss, it's not much, and way less than I used to wear, but it makes me feel more put together.

Fluffing my brown hair around my shoulders, I exhale a sigh. I'm sure I did, but I can't remember sighing before we lost Luna. It's like sometimes I hold my breath without realizing and when I let it go it's this mighty gust leaving me.

Slipping my feet into a pair of Vans I scoop up Will, give him a kiss, on his head, and put him back in his cage with a treat.

Downstairs, my parents are making breakfast together —my dad is preparing waffles, and my mom is cooking eggs and bacon.

"There you are." She turns and smiles over her shoulder. "I heard you moving around."

"Yeah, I was letting Will play while I got dressed."

"You look nice. Going somewhere with the boy next door?" My dad raises a brow, a challenge in his voice.

I roll my eyes playfully as I slide onto the stool and cross my right leg over the left. "No and no. But I did think I might go grab a coffee or smoothie or something."

"Do you need one of us to take you?" My mom asks. "You have your license, you're welcome to borrow one of the cars for a bit."

"Thanks, I might. Do you need help with anything?"

"Just put the plates on the table. We're almost done with all of this."

Someone looking in from the outside might think everything is normal, that my parents are already over Luna's death, but I know better. I see the sadness in both their eyes, or the times my dad disappears and I know he's left to drive around and cry to himself, or how my mom is cooking and baking incessantly to keep busy so she's not constantly reminded of the way she used to spend her time worrying about Luna and trying to make things easier for her.

That's the thing about grief, after a while people learn to mask it, but that doesn't mean it's not still there.

I hop up from the stool and distribute the plates and utensils on the table. Then I gather the syrup and butter, placing it in the middle so it's easy for all of us to get to.

My dad carries over a plate piled high with waffles that'll last a few days for the three of us. Luna, however, would've devoured as many as she could before our mom told her to stop.

Mom joins us with the eggs and bacon and we each pile a little of everything onto our plates.

"I think I'm going to try out for the play," I insert casually, taking a bite of waffle.

Their eyes swivel to me. "Really?" My dad sounds shocked, and for some reason I feel mildly offended by that fact.

I shrug, pushing the eggs around my plate. "I wasn't going to at first, but..." I hold off on finishing my thought of *Finn asked me to.*

"But?" My mom prompts.

"I thought it might be a good experience." It's not a total lie. If I get a part I'm sure it'll be a great experience, but that's not why I'm doing it.

"Oh." She smiles, crossing her fingers together. "I think it's an awesome idea."

"But you didn't do cheerleading this year." My clueless dad interjects.

"I wasn't interested." It's the easiest explanation since they don't know the true reason.

"Interests change," my mom pipes in. "And this is a very important time in your life. It's important to try new things." When I first spoke of joining theatre she didn't understand, but I'm glad now she seems to be on my side.

"Yeah, I guess so." My dad shrugs in agreement.

"I probably won't get a part anyway." I take another reluctant bite of food, it now sits in the pit of my stomach like a heavy and unyielding rock. "I'll probably just end up working on sets or something."

"Aw, honey, be optimistic."

I force a smile, and don't bother telling her I don't really want a part.

I know Mr. Rochester will only give me a part if he feels I'm deserving of it, in which case I'll accept, but it's not something I'm dying to do. If I end up benched, it won't hurt my feelings.

But I want to see Finn get a bigger part, to step out of his comfort zone and stop hiding in the background. If my auditioning gives him the support he needs, then I'll do it.

We finish breakfast and I clean everything up, stacking the dirty dishes in the dishwasher and turning it on, then also scrubbing the counters clean until they shine.

I didn't used to be bothered to do anything like this to help my parents. When it came to nights and weekends, I couldn't dash out of the house fast enough to meet up with friends. I was selfish, not uncaring, but my world definitely revolved around me.

I've finished when my mom pokes her head around the corner.

"Your dad and I are going out for a while. He wants to get a snow blower before it gets *really* cold." She rolls her eyes playfully. "Men and their toys. The keys to my car are on the counter."

I look over to the catch-all bowl and find her keys resting in it along with some change, a pack of gum, and a receipt.

"Thanks."

"Send one of us a text if you leave though, we ... we worry." Her face falls and once again I'm exhaling a deep heavy sigh, as if I'm weighted down by the burden I know she must feel.

"I will," I promise.

I still feel horrible about the first day I went to theatre club and forgot to let her know.

She nods and gives me a forced smile before she turns and leaves.

"Bye, Violet! We'll see you later!" I hear my dad call, and then within a minute or two they're gone.

Since it's still early, I decide to clean out Will Ferret's cage. My happy little ferret dances giddily through my room as I take apart his cage and dump the dirty bedding in a trash bag before I carefully scrub the bottom of the cage and fill it once more with clean fluffy bedding. Little tufts of whatever it's made of coat my floor like a downy snow. I grab the vacuum cleaner from the hall closet and

Will eagerly tries to play with it. I don't know why he likes it so much, I would assume most don't but maybe I'm wrong.

With my room spotless once more I return the vacuum to the closet and pick up Will, plopping on my bed with him cradled in my arms.

He burrows his pink nose against my neck and I giggle when his whiskers tickle me.

"Hey, bud." I rub the top of his head and I swear he smiles. "You're the cutest ferret ever. I know all ferret mom's probably think that, but I'm the only one who's right." I nuzzle my nose against his.

After a few more snuggles I tuck him back into his cage and he promptly climbs into his hammock.

I send a quick text to my mom, letting her know I'm leaving. I'm tempted to take the car, it'll be quicker and I'll have heat, but I know my days of using my bike are coming to an end until spring. I tuck my phone into my purse and deposit my purse into the basket before taking off.

Despite the cool temperature I stay plenty warm through the ride into town. I park my bike outside the coffee shop, leaning it against the brick exterior. I head inside the bustling coffee shop and wait in line to place my order for a latte.

Once it's in my hand, I start to leave, but a hesitant call of my name has me pausing before I can.

"Violet?" The voice calls again and my eyes land on a girl in a black turtleneck waving madly to get my attention.

I walk over, recognizing her from school but unable to put a name to the face.

"We're in theatre club together. I'm Lydia." Her inky black hair is tipped in blue and magenta tones. Her eyes are slanted and she has dark olive skin. If I had to guess her ethnicity I would say she's Vietnamese.

"Violet," I say before realizing what a ridiculous response it is since obviously she knows my name.

She smiles at me in clear amusement, but doesn't mock me. "I see you hanging out with Finn."

I nod, tucking a piece of hair behind my ear. I don't really know what she wants, since she's yet to ask a question.

The coffee shop continues to bustle with activity as I stand in front of her, waiting for more.

"Sit." Lydia points to an empty chair. "You don't have to keep standing there."

"Oh." I toss a thumb over my shoulder. "I was just getting coffee and heading home. I don't really have time to hang out."

Aka: I don't want to hang out. I don't even know you.

Her face falls a little and her eyes look sad, but she quickly returns to a smile. "That's okay. I'll see you at school then."

I walk out of the shop, confused and shaken by the awkward conversation. She's never said a word to me, and even though I know I've seen her around school there's not been any indication of her wanting to speak to me before.

I secure my coffee in the basket along with my bag and bike home as quickly as I can.

Spotting Finn sitting on his front porch stairs, I slow my bike and hop off.

Jack lies on the ground near Finn's worn black Converse shoes. Finn's dark blue eyes watch me from behind his glasses as I approach, my latte clasped between both hands so I can finish it before it gets too cold.

"Chai tea latte?" He looks up at me, squinting to see me against the sun behind me.

I can't stop my grin as I take a slow sip and nod. "You remembered?"

He shrugs and scoots over, silently offering me a place to sit beside him. I perch my butt on the wooden stairs, our bodies so close that our clothes brush against each other with every movement.

"I would've brought you something," I tell him, knocking my knee against his playfully. He doesn't retreat and it feels like some sort of small win. "I wasn't sure what you were up to today."

"It's okay," he murmurs, staring ahead.

"Have any plans?"

He shakes his head, his dark hair tumbling into his eyes. "My mom's working so..."

"So, you're home alone?" I raise a brow.

He nods, looking down at his sneakers.

"Do you ... want to come to my house?"

I wouldn't normally invite a boy over to my house without my parents being there, but this is Finn and the chances of something happening are slim to none.

Even if I want to kiss him more than anything.

The thought hits me like a ton of bricks collapsing on top of me, but it's true. More and more I'm imagining how his lips would feel against mine. Would they be pillow soft? Or firm? Would he hold my cheeks, or just stand there? Would he even want to kiss me or is it nothing but a far off hope for me?

"Do you want me to come to your house?" I'm surprised by his counter, but from the look of disbelief on his face I know he's probably never been invited to a friend's house.

"Sure. My parents won't mind."

"Now?"

"Now's fine."

He stands up and Jack instantly rises with him. Despite the fact Jack isn't wearing his service vest today he's clearly in tune with everything Finn does.

He follows me over to my house where I enter the garage code and wheel my bike inside. He watches the garage door go down after I push the button.

"You coming?" I ask, my hand on the door to the inside.

His head swivels back to me. "Can I see your ferret?"

I grin, my cheeks coloring. I don't know why it makes me so ridiculously happy that he remembered my ferret.

"Come on, this way."

Once inside, I head for the stairs to my room, but when I don't hear the echo of his steps behind me I turn around to look.

Finn stands at the bottom of the staircase, both hands shoved into the pockets of his jeans, with Jack at his side tongue lolling out.

"What's wrong?" My hand hovers over the bannister.

"Will Jack scare Will? Maybe this is a bad idea." His

eyes dart around the unfamiliar space, his shoulders tight with unease.

I turn back around and descend the steps, stopping on the second to last one. His eyes meet mine for the briefest of seconds before he stares at my nose and then looks at his shoes.

"Jack won't bother Will, I promise. Will's used to other animals."

"But Jack is big and ferrets are small."

I smile, itching to brush his tousled hair away from his forehead. "We had a dog a couple of years ago. Jack is nothing Will can't handle, and much better behaved than the wild dog we had." I can tell Finn is still unsure, but I stick out my pinky finger. "Come on," I urge, wiggling my finger.

He presses his lips together and then smiles, and that smile alone makes my entire stomach flip and turn, exploding with butterflies.

His finger hooks in mine and he follows behind me up the steps. Jack sprints past us and stops at the landing, tail wagging.

Our fingers don't drop as I lead him down the hall to my bedroom. I ease the door open and pause as he gets his first look at my bedroom.

"This is ... my room." It's an unnecessary statement, but one I make anyway.

His eyes roam over every bit. From the walls, to my bed, dresser, desk, and even the floor. I don't think he misses a single detail. He finally let's go and walks over to the wall where I stuck up my photos. He hones in on one and points.

"Your sister." It's a statement, not a question.

I walk up beside him and look at the photo he's pointing to. It's Luna and I, Christmas morning when I was twelve and she was nine. We're in matching red and green plaid flannel pajamas. I stand behind her with my arms wrapped around her. Horrendous blunt bangs cover my forehead and my hair sticks up with static. Braces cover my teeth and baby fat still rounds my cheeks. Luna's hair is long and curly. Her head is tilted back, smiling up at me like I'm her whole world. It's one of my favorite pictures of us.

"This is a more recent one." I point to another of me dressed up for spirit day at school. Luna and I pose outside our old house—*my* old house, considering it's the only home she ever knew—our backs are to each other and we're making finger guns like Charlie's Angels.

"You look different," Finn muses. He continues to study all my photos.

"How?" I prompt. "How do I look different?"

"Your eyes." His fingers touch the edge of a photo of me laughing on a swing set with one of my old friends. "They're different now."

He turns away from the photo and faces me. He's probably pushing six feet tall, so he's plenty taller than me. I have to tilt my head back to face him, but I don't mind. His eyes scan my face, but never meet my own icy blue hues.

"Tell me how they look." My voice is soft, shaky. He

steps closer to me and my breath catches with an embarrassing gasp.

He reaches out and I hold the air in my lungs as he grabs a piece of my hair between his fingers. He rubs it between his thumb and forefinger, puzzlement on his face as if he's trying to decide whether he likes the feel of it or not.

"They look..." His eyes zero in on my lips and I involuntarily lick them. "They look like a raging arctic sea. Like there shouldn't be hope for getting to the other side, but there is. What gives you hope, Violet?"

"Laughing with my mom in the kitchen," I whisper in answer. "Movie nights with my parents. Appreciating the simplest things as if I'm only witnessing them for the first time. But I find the most hope in a meadow beneath the stars with the boy next door." His lips quirk and tears sting my eyes. "With you, Finn. I find *hope* with you. It's not the wishes we need, right?" I choke. "It's the hope." I reach out unwillingly, grasping the fabric of his shirt in my hands. He straightens, but doesn't pull away.

"Why me?" I guess it's his turn for a question, rightfully so.

"Why not you?" I counter, my fingers flexing against his sides.

"You're too good for someone like me. You deserve someone better. Someone normal. Someone who can look you in the eye." He swallows thickly, his Adam's apple bobbing.

"I *choose* you."

"Why?"

"Because I can."

Before I can give myself a second to think, because I know I'll change my mind, I stand on my tiptoes, cupping his jaw in my hand as I angle his mouth to mine. I press my lips to his and he's frozen against me. His hands don't touch me. His lips don't even move at first. But then he melts against me, his body turning from ice to fluid. Hesitant hands touch my cheeks and he kisses me back gently.

There is no tongue, it's not the wild passionate kissing you see in movies, but it's perfect nonetheless.

Letting him go, I step back and he raises shaky fingers to his lips.

"You kissed me."

It's not a question, but I answer anyway.

"I did."

"Why?" He lets his fingers drop to his side. His eyes are wide behind his glasses, stunned and in complete disbelief.

"Because I choose you," I repeat. "Because I can." I exhale a shaky breath and give him a small hesitant smile. "Because I want to."

"You shouldn't want me." He shakes his head.

"But I do."

"I'm not good for you."

"Finn—" I start to argue, but he shuts me down with a change of subject.

"I want to see your ferret. I came to see him. To see Will. I didn't come here to see you. The ferret. I want to see him." He's breathless as he blurts out each short sentence with a jerky but firm hand, his eyes glued to the wood floor beneath our feet.

"R-Right," I stutter, stepping further away from him. Any warmth I felt a moment before being so close to him is gone, only icy cold in its place.

I pad across my room to Will's cage and he runs eagerly to get let out. I scoop him into my arms and face Finn.

"Finn, meet Will Ferret. Will Ferret, this is Finn."

Finn smiles, cocking his head to the side as he assesses the little creature in my arms.

"Nice to meet you, Will." He reaches out and gently shakes my ferret's tiny paw. "I'm sorry Violet gave you such a horrible."

"It's not horrible." I jut my lower lip out in defense. "Do you want to hold him?"

He looks down at Jack and back at me. "Jack might get jealous."

"How about this, I'll snuggle Jack while you play with Will so he doesn't feel left out?"

He ponders my words and shrugs his shoulders. "Okay."

He holds his hands out and I hand over Will. He laughs when Will wiggles against his face.

"He's soft."

"And a wiggle worm," I add, dropping to my knees so I can scratch Jack behind his ears. He hardly seems jealous, but I want to assuage Finn's worries.

"I like him," he announces.

"Ferrets are cool little creatures. I call him a sausage hamster," I confess, laughter lilting my voice.

"Why?" His brows furrow. "He's a ferret. Not a hamster."

Sometimes I forget how literal Finn takes things, but it doesn't bother me. It just gives me more of a chance to talk to him.

"Yeah, I know, it's just a silly thing, you know because hamsters are short but he's long like a sausage link."

"Oh," he replies, but I know he still doesn't think it makes much sense.

He snuggles Will for a few more minutes before he passes him back over. I tuck Will back into his cage and Finn follows me downstairs, Jack trailing behind him. He stands in the foyer with his hands in his pockets. Like in my room, his eyes drift around, landing on every surface like he wants to memorize the exact items and their placement in my home.

I'm not ready to say goodbye. It's silly, but it's true, so I blurt, "It's almost lunchtime. Would you want to stay?"

"Stay?"

"For lunch." I clear my throat, fearing my cheeks are blazing pink. I can't stop thinking about the kiss. It was simple, but perfect. However, I can't help but be worried about his reaction. He's acting like nothing happened, but I'm sure he hasn't forgotten it. Finn seems to have an endless memory when it comes to everything.

He twists his lips back and forth in thought, looks behind him at the door, and finally at me. I expect him to say he has to go, but he doesn't.

"Lunch would be nice."

A huge smile breaks across my face, my heart soaring my chest. "Come on, I'll start making us sandwiches."

He follows me into the kitchen and I point for him to sit on one of the stools. He doesn't, instead he roams through the kitchen picking up knick-knacks and studying them before returning them to the exact spot and position they were in previously. I pull out ingredients for a sandwich and look at him over my shoulder.

"Turkey, cool? What do you want on it?"

He pauses, toying with a pen from my dad's job between his fingers.

"I like turkey."

"What do you want on it?" I ask again.

He puts the pen down, his tongue sliding out briefly to wet his lips. "Tomato, lettuce, onion, and mayonnaise."

"You got it." I start getting everything cut up and ready to put together. "Ugh," I complain, wiping my eyes with the sleeve of my shirt. "Why do onions make you cry? This is the worst."

It's a rhetorical question, but Finn answers anyway, spinning away from one of the pantry cabinets that has the school calendar taped to it with important events and days off.

"Onions produce a chemical irritant. It stimulates your tear ducts and that's why you cry." He pauses by the island and grabs an orange from the wooden bowl, spinning it around and looking for imperfections in the surface.

"Good to know." I finish with the onions and wash my

hands before I grab a tissue and clean my eyes free of stinging tears.

All that's left is to build our sandwiches, so I do that and pull several bags of chips from the pantry.

"Pick your poison, " I joke, spreading the options on the counter.

"Huh?" A brow peaks and he looks at me in confusion.

"Pick which one you want," I clarify.

He bites his lip and seems to be weighing his options seriously. Finally he reaches out and picks the Cool Ranch Doritos snack size pack.

"Good choice." I put the other two away and grab another Doritos pack for myself.

We carry our plates over to the table and he sits down across from me.

"This is ... nice, Violet."

"I hope it's good." I take a bite, and immediately have to wipe mayonnaise from the corner of my lip. We both chuckle and the easy camaraderie is nice, but I still wish I knew what he thought of the kiss.

Did I just take him by surprise? Did he not like it? Or does he just not want to kiss *me?*

But I can't ask him any of those questions. Not because he's autistic, but because I like him. When you like a boy, rejection is scary and sucks. He already seemed flustered about the kiss. I don't want to have to force him to tell me he doesn't like me in that way. I'd rather be his friend than nothing at all.

He takes a bite of chip, crunching on it as he looks out

the back window of the kitchen at the deck and the meadow beyond.

His gaze slowly drift backs to me. "Will I see you tonight?"

I try to suppress the butterflies assaulting my stomach, because his question means nothing. "Probably," I answer, even though it's *most definitely*.

"Good," he muses, looking outside again. "Would you want to look through my telescope?"

"That sounds fun." I grab a napkin from the holder on the table and wipe my hands.

"Telescopes are like a portal," he replies softly, his head downcast with his eyes on his plate. "They show you a whole other world, that down here you think surely can't exist. But it does. It's out there. It's real. As real as you or me. Whatever happens to us, to Earth, that's always going to exist in some way. Space is infinite. We don't know how far it goes, what's truly out there, none of it."

"Do you think there are aliens?" I can't help joking with him.

"I think it's naïve to think we're the only intelligent life form to exist. I believe life exists in some way out there, we just haven't found it yet. If outer space is infinite, isn't life, therefore, infinite too?" He tilts his head to the side. "Or at least the possibility of it? You can't rule out other lives until you've explored all those galaxies, planets, on and on. The mistake we make as humans is thinking other life means exactly like us and what we know. Life can be anything. Even bacteria is alive."

"Wow." I'm taken aback by his speech.

He looks out the window, toward the sky now. "One day I'll be up there. I'll see it all. Experience it. The awe. The beauty."

I hope more than anything he does get that experience. He deserves it more than anyone I know.

"I believe you." My voice is barely above a whisper as I choke on emotion. I want that for him. I want it more than anything.

"No one else does."

"I do." I reach across the table, extending my pinky, and after a short hesitation he returns the gesture. "Prove them wrong, Finn."

His eyes meet mine.

One second.

Two.

Three—

They drop.

"I will."

CHAPTER EIGHTEEN

I WATCH OUT THE WINDOW FOR FINN TO COME outside. It's not like this is any different than usual. I wait for him lots of nights, but somehow this feels bigger than those nights.

When I finally see him step outside, it's my cue to leave.

I'm already dressed warmly, my feet stuffed into a pair of fuzzy boots.

I slip outside and into the dark, carefully making my way from our yard to his, up the deck, to stop in front of him beside his giant telescope.

It's huge, not like anything I've ever seen before. I've noticed it from my house, but up close it's even bigger, almost the size of me. Holding out a hesitant hand, my palm hovers above the edge of the telescope.

Letting my hand drop back to my side I face Finn.

"Hi."

Why does this boy make me so ridiculously awkward?

"Hi." His voice echoes into the night, the faintest hint of his breath fogging the air. "You can ... you can look." He sweeps his hand toward the telescope.

I want to tell him I am looking. I'm looking at him, and as long as I'm looking at him I don't need a night full of stars. He's brighter than them all, he just can't see it.

I don't say any of that. Instead, I lower my head and peer through the lens. A gasp emits from my throat. I've never looked through a telescope and it's nothing like I would've expected. It's...

"Magic," I whisper.

"Magic doesn't exist. This does."

My body tingles, tightening when I feel the barest pressure of Finn's fingertips against my back.

"It's beautiful," I murmur, and it is. "W-What's that I'm seeing?" I try to point with my finger in the night sky to what I see through the telescope.

"Saturn," he answers, his voice close to my ear. His presence is all around me. I'm consumed by it. Lost in him.

Drowning.

Not too long ago I wanted to drown in memories. Now I just want to drown in Finn.

"It's incredible."

I'm running out of adjectives, but the view through the lens is so astounding that adequate words fail me.

"Let me show you something else." His feather light touch leaves me as I step away from the telescope.

He does some adjustments with knobs and buttons that mean absolutely nothing to me.

"Now look."

It's dark, but I feel his eyes on me. I feel like he's not just seeing the outer shell, but every single thought, emotion, and my very soul. It's all in the intensity of his gaze. His body language. It's so much more than a simple look.

I step up to the telescope once more.

"Oh, my God! Finn! This is incredible!" My exclamation is much too loud for the late hour, but he doesn't shush me. I can feel happiness radiating off of him like this very real, tangible thing I can just reach out and grab.

I can see the rings around Saturn. Clearly. Fully. It's magnificent.

"I see why you want to go to outer space now."

It's impossible to deny the majesty of seeing the planet so clearly. I never cared to see any of them with my own eye. Beyond a picture in a textbook I couldn't tell you what they looked like, let alone recall them to memory, but this? I will never forget this.

"Thank you for sharing this with me." I stand up from my hunched position behind the lens and face him.

He nods, a small dip of his head.

He may not voice it, but I know this has to be a big deal for him.

The stars, space, the infinite realms beyond are his safe place. When he looks at them he can imagine any number of lives, all of them where he's someone who isn't judged simply for existing.

Stepping away from the telescope I expect him to take my place, but instead he surprises me by holding out his pinky finger. I hook mine with his and he leads me off the deck and through the yard until we reach the meadow.

He tilts his head back, looking above. Our fingers are still hooked together and I have no intention of dropping his.

"My best memories happen under the night sky," he murmurs.

Hesitantly, I rest my head on his shoulder. He stiffens for a solid ten seconds before he relaxes.

"I don't know what I would've done if I hadn't met you." The words are a low murmur, a quiet admission of my heart.

"You would've been fine."

"I'm not so sure." I exhale a shaky breath, fighting tears that burn the back of my eyes.

"You're a fighter, Nebula. You don't need anyone." *I may not need anyone but I want you.* "Can I try something?"

I straighten and he turns to face me, our fingers falling from each other. "Try what?"

His eyes drop to the ground and he toes the dirt, his hands shoved into his pockets.

"Finn?" I coax, my fingers grazing his cheek lightly, encouraging him to look at me.

He shakes his head back and forth and rocks on his heels.

"Finn," I laugh softly, "come on, tell me. It's okay."

His lips twist together, his dark hair tumbling over his forehead and shielding his eyes further from me.

"I ... I ... I want to try t-to," his hands twitch at his sides with nerves and I want to steady them, remind him it's okay, but I know his ticks help him cope with uncomfortable situations and for whatever reason he's bothered by something, "to ... *kissyouagain*."

He rushes the last words together, slurring them, but I still hear them and I'm unable to stop the tiny gasp that rushes through my lips.

"But I thought—" I stop myself and shake my head. Maybe he didn't dislike the kiss as much as I believed he did. "I would like that," I say instead of finishing my first thought.

He nods and steps closer to me until our shoes are toe to toe.

My heart drums a raucous beat.

"Hold still," he commands in a soft voice, eyes on my lips.

I resist the urge to lick my lips and close my eyes.

Seconds tick by, maybe longer, and my heart lurches into my throat when I feel the tender press of his mouth to mine. A moment later his hands cup my cheeks, but barely, almost hovering against me like he's scared to touch me.

I stay still, despite the urge to touch him, knowing he needs to be in control of this so I give him that.

His lips move hesitantly against mine, nervously studying the contour.

When he steps away, slightly breathless, I think he's

taken my heart with him because I can't feel it beating anymore.

"Did I do it right?" The slight hesitation in his voice makes me sad.

I nod, still stunned from the feel of his kiss.

He grins and it's as blinding as the sun.

I stare at him, the stars shining behind him, and feel myself falling.

It's in that moment that I know my life has been irrevocably changed by Finnley Crawford and I don't ever want it to go back.

CHAPTER NINETEEN

"All right, shut your mouths, it's audition time," Mr. Rochester announces, waving his hands for us to quiet down.

Conversation ceases to exist because you *always* listen to Mr. Rochester.

He's probably the one teacher in the entire school everyone is afraid of but also respects immensely.

He strides across the lit stage, pausing in the middle to assess our group.

Beside me, Finn squirms in his seat and Jack rests his head on Finn's knee in comfort.

"If you've signed up to audition," he taps his pen against the clipboard clasped in his hand, "then you'll come up when I call your name. Don't be nervous, you all make fool's of yourselves on the daily anyway. Any questions?" He waits and when no one raises their hand he takes it as an answer. "Let's begin. First up, Luanne Dane."

We sit back and watch her audition, then the next, and another.

So on it goes until my name is called. I silently curse Finn in my head for talking me into this, but I also know this is the exact thing I need to do. If we don't push our boundaries then life becomes unbearably stagnant.

I scoot past Finn and stride down the aisle, ignoring the feel of too many eyes on me.

Up the stairs to the stage where I had lunch with Finn I pause in the spot where Mr. Rochester stood when he came in. He now sits in the first row, clipboard balanced on his knee, waiting.

"Any time, Ms. Page."

I take a deep breath, trying to calm my nerves. My hands shake so badly that the script in my hands is noticeably unsteady.

I search the seats until I find Finn.

Centering myself, I begin.

I let everything else fade to the background. There's just me, the stage beneath my feet, the words leaving my mouth, and Finn.

I finish and Mr. Rochester gives a single nod. His face is neutral, giving absolutely nothing away about whether or not I did okay.

I sit back down beside Finn, expelling a breath I didn't know I was holding.

"You were brilliant, Nebula."

I look over in surprise at his hushed tone. "Really?"

He nods. "I wouldn't lie."

"I know you wouldn't. But I thought I did horribly."

He shakes his head. "No, you were magnetic."

Before I can think I lean over and kiss his cheek. He stiffens in surprise and I pull away hastily.

"I-I'm sorry. I didn't think."

He touches his long fingers to his cheek. "I ... liked it."

I smile, opening my mouth to speak but his name is called.

"Good luck," I whisper as he gets up, Jack following at his heels.

Somehow as Finn gets on stage I'm even more nervous for him than I was myself, which is silly considering he's done this before and I'm the newbie.

Watching him give his audition I'm in complete awe. He gives it his all, becoming a whole new person, like he's stepped into another dimension and is tapping into someone else's thoughts and feelings. He *is* the character. There is no stuttering or hesitation with him. He's playing a role and in it he's comfortable embracing the character's personality and persona. Finn doesn't exist in that moment, only the character.

When he finishes a few tears cascade down my cheeks and I hastily wipe them away, schooling my features so he isn't confused by my reaction.

He sits down beside me once more, completely unruffled by what he did up there.

I can't find any words to speak to express how amazing he did, so I say nothing instead. Words wouldn't be adequate anyway.

The auditions wind down and since there's still time left Mr. Rochester puts us all to work on building and painting the sets.

Finn and I sequester ourselves in a corner, painting the front of Belle's house that the woodshop class made.

I dip the paintbrush in white and work on the siding while Finn paints the door blue.

We work in silence, focused on the task at hand.

A shadow descends over us and I feel Finn stiffen.

Looking up I find Lydia standing there with a nervous smile.

"Um … hi. Mind if I join you guys?"

I look to Finn for his answer. He looks away and returns to painting the door in up and down strokes.

"I guess so," I mumble, eyeing him for any sign of tightening in his shoulders or body. There is none.

She grabs another paintbrush and dips it in white, helping me with the siding since that's the biggest task at hand.

"Thanks for letting me work with you guys." The words are a whispered slur under her breath like she's afraid to release them.

"Why *do* you want to work with us?"

She looks at me and Finn behind me. "Because I'm tired of people pretending to be my friend and then whispering about me behind my back. I don't want to be something I'm not for people to like me. I admire that about you."

"Thanks?" It comes out as a question and she laughs.

"It's a good thing, believe me. It's a breath of fresh air.

This school is a bunch of cliqueish snobs, all too eager to spend mommy and daddy's money and step on anyone they can to get where they're going. I ... I moved here my sophomore year and I've wanted nothing more than to be one of them, but I'm not, I never will be and for the first time I'm *happy* I'm not like them. But I could still use friends."

"Oh." I'm surprised to say the least. Her words weren't what I was expecting.

"I know you don't really know me yet," her smile is shy and she tucks a strand of black straight hair behind her ear, "but I'm hoping we can be friends." She looks at Finn too.

"That would be ... nice."

I wasn't planning on making any friends. But then Finn happened, so who am I to say no to Lydia? She's clearly craving a real friendship and if you don't give something a try you never know. If I cast her aside it doesn't make me any better than those girls I hate, even the ghost of myself.

Her smile turns from shy and hesitant to relieved and we focus on painting.

A little while later Mr. Rochester dismisses us, calling after our retreating figures that casting will be posted by the end of the week.

Nerves surge through me once more, but I shrug them off. I have no control over this and whatever happens is what's meant to be.

Lydia walks with Finn and I out of the school and then waves goodbye as she heads to her car.

Finn releases a breath and I frown.

"Are you okay? If Lydia bothers you that's okay."

"I don't like change." He squints at the sun above us. "But you've changed me and I like it so I should give her a chance too. Having friends isn't as bad as I thought it would be."

I beam at his words. "You've changed me too."

"I have?" He glances at me in shock before his eyes dart to the sidewalk beneath him, always careful not to step on any cracks.

"Yeah." I clasp my backpack straps in my hands. "I can't quite explain it, but you have. I see things with new eyes."

"But your eyes are the same," he states.

I laugh, a full belly laugh that fills my whole body with joy. "Not literally, Finn."

"Oh, right. You were kidding." He gives me a half-smile, his lips crooked on one side and that's when I know he wasn't being serious but playing with me instead.

"You suck." I playfully bump him with my shoulder and he laughs too.

We reach his car and he lets Jack in the back.

I slide in the passenger seat and Finn gets behind the wheel.

We look at each other, smiling like goofballs.

When I first started talking to him, the ease and camaraderie we share now felt like a far off dream, but now it's a reality and I don't want to look back.

CHAPTER TWENTY

My nerves are shot come Friday. The casting sheet is supposed to be posted today. I'm torn between wanting a major part and nothing at all. I honestly don't know which will make me happy and which I'll be disappointed over.

"Don't you want breakfast, Vi?" My mom calls after me as I hurry down the stairs and toward the door.

I look back at her over my shoulder. "I'm not hungry."

My stomach is upset from worry and I don't see myself managing to keep down the scrambled eggs and bacon I can smell wafting from the kitchen.

"Are you sure?" She stands in the entryway, wiping her hands on a dishtowel.

"Really, I'm fine, Mom. Just worried about the audition is all, and it's making me not have much of an appetite."

She nods, appeased by my answer. "Good luck." She smiles reassuringly, but it doesn't ease the tightening in my chest.

"Thanks."

I slip outside and start down the path and across the driveway to Finn's house next door.

I stop short when his car is gone.

My brows furrow in confusion. It doesn't seem like Finn to leave me here and not tell me. My worry deepens, not about the play, but in concern. What if something happened to Finn? He could be hurt or—well, that doesn't make sense because I doubt he'd be in his car if that were the case.

I turn around to head back to my house and ask my mom for a ride since it's too cold to take my bike when I see his car turn down the street. He pulls up in front of my driveway and I walk up to the driver's side as he rolls down the window.

I bend down, fighting a smile. "Did you forget me?"

He looks at me in panic. "N-No, I didn't forget you. I wouldn't do that. I-I wanted to surprise you."

"Surprise me?" I blurt, taken aback. "What do you mean?"

"I know you're nervous about the casting so..."

His eyes drop to his lap and he pushes his glasses up his nose.

"Yes?" I prompt when he's still quiet.

He takes a deep breath. "I went to get you a chai tea latte and chocolate croissant."

Words flee from me. I stare at him dumbfounded. "You

mean to tell me you got up early, drove to the coffee shop, and went inside during peak time to get me a latte and croissant?"

"Y-Yes," he stutters. He only stutters when he's feeling nervous or unsure of himself, and I don't want him to feel either.

"Finn." Tears prick my eyes. "That's the sweetest thing anyone has ever done for me."

The fact that he braved the crowded coffee shop in order to bring me something to brighten my day and ease my stress is just ... *wow*. I have no words.

"I did good?" He shakes his head, wetting his lips and gives me a small smile. "I'm not ... I don't know how to do this."

"Well, you're doing a perfectly good job. We better get going."

He nods in agreement and rolls up his window as I cross in front of the car, climbing in beside him.

I wasn't hungry for bacon and eggs but I eagerly grab the bag containing the croissant—pleased to see he got one for himself—and pull off a bite.

"Mmm, this is delicious," I hum, closing my eyes as the delicious chocolate chips melt on my tongue.

Happiness rolls off of him and his easy smile is almost too much for my heart to handle.

"Thank you." I lean over and kiss his cheek.

His face reddens. "Y-You're welcome."

He turns the car around and we head for the school. We both finish our croissants before he parks, and we each take our drinks with us.

I'm still blown away that he went and did this. That wasn't a little thing for him to do. There are no words to convey how proud I am of him, but also how much it means to me.

Finn holds the door open for me going inside and the nerves that had calmed with his sweet gesture skyrocket. I have no control over the outcome, whether I get a big part, small, or none at all. I have to roll with what happens, but that doesn't ease my anxiety.

Finn hooks his finger with mine and we stroll down the hall, him practically leading the way with his long-legged gait, to the board where the casting will be posted.

"Hey, guys! Wait up!" Lydia calls after us, running down the hall. Her backpack slaps against her body as she hurries.

Finn and I pause, giving her a chance to catch up. While Finn and I still relatively stick to ourselves, Lydia has hung out with us some this week, and she's not so bad. I think Finn is starting to warm up to her. I know he's hesitant, not trusting other people's motives, and I understand it completely. When it feels like everyone is against you it becomes difficult to trust genuine people.

"Thanks, guys." Lydia gives a small, relieved smile. "What part are you hoping for?" She directs the question to both of us.

"I don't know if I even want a part."

"Really?" Finn's head whips in my direction. "Why not?"

"I don't know if I could do it justice. I'm not exactly an actress or anything."

"I feel you," Lydia agrees, her pace matching ours. "I told Mr. Rochester I was fine with a small role, but nothing else. I'd rather work on costumes."

"Do you sew?"

She lights up, her whole face beaming with excitement. "Yes, and I love designing. That's what I'm hoping to do when I graduate. I'd love to work on movie sets designing the costumes. I love a challenge."

"Wow, that's impressive."

"Why?" Finn blurts. "It's just clothes."

I elbow him in the side lightly, but Lydia laughs.

"Finn has no filter."

"I've noticed. It's refreshing."

"I don't mean to be rude." Finn drops his head in shame and I instantly feel bad for picking on him.

"No, no, I like it," Lydia rushes to assure him.

"Me too," I agree.

We turn the corner and I see the bulletin board at the end of the hall.

My finger drops from Finn's as I quickly grab ahold of his whole hand. My grasp is tight, but somehow he manages to give me a reassuring squeeze.

We reach the board and Lydia breathes a sigh of relief. "No part for me, thank God."

"Why'd you try out then?" Finn asks curiously.

Lydia shrugs and steps aside. "To push my boundaries, I guess."

Finn nods and gives my hand one last silent reminder of his support before we both scan the list for our names.

"That can't be right." The words are muttered under

my breath in complete and utter disbelief. I read the list again, but my name is still in the same spot, and Finn's...

"Holy fucking shit," I blurt, blinking over and over until my vision begins to blur.

Finn grins down at me and presses a kiss to my cheek, practically on my lips. "Hello, Beauty."

I exhale a breath of disbelief and smile back at him. "Beast."

CHAPTER TWENTY-ONE

Time passes in a haze of studying, learning lines, practices, and stolen moments with Finn. With Thanksgiving only days away there's still no label on our relationship. I know what I want, but I don't know how to ask him. Approaching the subject of asking if he wants to be my boyfriend leaves me with a lump of fear in my stomach. We kiss on occasion, hold hands, but beyond that it's completely innocent.

I wrap my fingers around the warm cup of coffee as Finn and I cross the street from the coffee shop to his car. The snow on the ground is mushy and gray, but still several inches deep. My snow boots are covered in grime and look like they've seen several years of use versus only about a month and a half.

Finn let's Jack hop in the back, then climbs in and

starts the car, letting the heat pour inside. We weren't in the shop more than fifteen minutes ordering and waiting for our coffee and treats but the car is ice cold already. My breath fogs the air inside the car as we wait for it to warm. I bring my drink to my lips, letting it heat me from the inside.

Finn tugs his beanie lower over his ears. He looks adorably rumpled in his puffy coat and jeans. His beanie is loose, hiding most of his curly black hair. Like always, his glasses are slipping down his nose and right on cue he pushes them up and back into place.

"Are you and your mom doing anything for Thanksgiving?"

He smells his coffee and takes a sip before answering. "My brother and sister are coming." He wrinkles his nose and I don't know whether it's because of the smell or irritation about his siblings.

"That sounds nice."

"Eh." He shrugs with his noncommittal noise.

"Not a fan?" I arch a brow and he twists his lips in thought.

"They don't ... understand me. Not like you do." He turns to me, his blue eyes dark and serious. They're a dangerous swirl of ocean and the midnight blue of darkness. "I wish everyone saw things like you."

"Most people are too closed-minded." I shrug, kicking my feet up on the dashboard and looking across at the ice rink that's been erected in the center of town.

Out of the corner of my eye I see him lean his head

back against the seat. "Tell me something about your sister. Something little or big. Just anything."

It doesn't take me long to think of something and a smile comes with the memory. "She loved crayons. A new box of crayons was literally her favorite thing in the world. She loved coloring pictures. Her whole room was covered in pictures she colored or drew. She was constantly leaving them for my parents and me." A wistful sigh leaves my lips.

It's heartbreaking to know I'll never have a colored pictured of Barbie or a Disney princess left for me again. Those were her favorite, but I did get the occasional Star Wars character now and then. The last Christmas before she passed my parents got her a bunch of those fancy adult coloring books with the intricate designs. Although she could color them fine, she didn't like them.

"It would've been nice if I could've met her."

I swivel my head in his direction, feeling the ache of my sister's loss deepen in my chest. "Yeah, it would've been."

I notice he doesn't say he *wishes* he could've met her. Wishes to Finn are nothing but a fairytale and I guess that's true. You can wish on a star, on a hope, a dream, but that doesn't will your desire into existence.

Picking an invisible piece of lint from my jeans, I avoid his gaze.

Finn, I know, would never look at me with pity, but I still fear seeing it in his eyes. Pity is the last thing I want. Pity doesn't bring her back, or change the way I feel. Pity is a cage.

Taking another sip of coffee, I drop my feet down, and ask, "Can we go to the bookstore?"

He grins—that adorable, dorkish, smile of his I love so much. "You think you can brave the cold?"

I stick my tongue out at him. "You grew up here. You're used to it. Come to Texas and see how you handle the heat, then we'll talk."

"Maybe one day," he murmurs, turning the car off. We get out, Jack following, and trek through the cold down the street to the bookstore—passing the smoothie place I frequented often in the summer.

Finn reaches the door and opens it as someone is about to come out.

"Oh." Lydia jolts backwards. "Hi, guys."

"Hey." I smile in surprise.

A plastic bag dangles from her fingers with a book.

"Uh ... hi," Finn mutters, staring at his shoes. Jack nudges his leg with his nose and Finn pets the top of his head. Finn doesn't dislike Lydia, but he still hasn't quite warmed to her. But it took him a while to get used to me too, so I think he'll get there.

"Are you enjoying break?" Lydia asks, shuffling to the side.

"Yeah, I am. It's been quiet so far."

Lydia nods. "Well, maybe we can hang out some over break. I know it's not a long one, but..." She runs her fingers through her long straight black hair. "To be honest, my whole family is in and when I say my whole family, I mean it. There are like fifty people hanging around on a daily basis."

"That sounds killer," I agree, while beside me Finn gives a noncommittal sound of agreement. "I'm sure we can do something. You can just come over and hang out if you want. I'll text you my address. We don't have any crazy plans, so any time would work."

She smiles widely. "That'd be awesome. Bye, guys!" In much better spirits than she was before, she waves and heads down the street.

"Close that door," Pete scolds. "I'm not paying to heat the outdoors."

"Sorry, Pete," I apologize as the two of us, and Jack step fully into the store and let the door swing closed behind us.

"Mhmm, sure you are," he hums, trying to hide a carefree smile.

Finn is already browsing the shelves, in search of something new to read. He devours books and is constantly in need of more. I don't really have a purpose in being here this time, except not being ready to go home.

I look around anyway, picking up a book here or there. I stop when I pull out a book of poems. The cover is simple, a cobalt blue with a silver squiggly line, and the title. Opening it, I scan some of the poems, one after the other speaking right to my soul.

"You want that?"

"Oh my God!" I cry, startled by the sound of Finn's voice right beside my ear. The book goes flying through the air and lands on the ground.

He picks it up and looks at the page it's open to. "*And in the darkness she found a light ... a beating heart ... a echo of her own.*" He rubs his lips together and shrugs. "Interesting. You want this?" He repeats.

I nod woodenly, still shocked by his sudden appearance. He tucks it under his arm along with three books he's pulled for himself. "I'm getting it for you."

"You don't have to do that," I protest, breaking free of my surprise.

"I want to." It's such a simple response, but from Finn it feels like the whole world.

It's silly, I know, but I can't help feeling the way I do.

"You ready?" he asks, his eyes scanning the shelf behind me.

"Mhmm." I nod, wringing my fingers together because I feel suddenly weird with nothing to hold in my hands.

"Come on, Jack." Finn heads to checkout and I trail behind him, still surprised he wants to buy the book for me.

After everything is rung up and paid, Pete bids us to have a good day, and we walk back through the frigid cold to his car once more.

Finn starts the car, but doesn't pull out right away. "I ... I realize I must've upset you—asking about your sister."

"You didn't upset me," I insist.

"No, I did, and I'm sorry. I'm not ... I'm not good at this." He looks at me briefly. "I don't understand social cues and nuisances. I ask questions and don't think about the consequences, for that, I'm sorry."

"Finn, I don't care that you asked about my sister." He opens his mouth to argue. "Truly." I place a hand over my heart. "It's the thoughts, the memories, that make me sad—

not your questions. Remembering is painful, but forgetting her is even more terrifying. The pain thoughts of her bring are the only thing that feels real anymore when it comes to her. Where there was joy there's only loss and hurt now."

"It scares me," he whispers, clasping the steering wheel tightly in hands. He still makes no move to back out.

"What does?"

"That I might never feel that for someone. I feel like I can't love like a normal person, so I probably can't grieve like one either. What if my mom died and I didn't miss her? That makes me a monster."

"You're not a monster, Finn." I reach over, cupping his cheek in my hand. His skin has the barest hint of stubble. "You're human. That's it."

His Adam's apple bobs as he swallows and his wary, tear-filled eyes slowly make their way to me. "You make me question *everything*." His voice becomes raw and gravely. My belly fills with an ache. A need.

In the blink of an eye I close the distance between us.

I kiss him, trying to will him to absorb my thoughts and feelings, so he can experience first hand how wonderful he is from my perspective. He kisses me back, desperation clinging to his lips. We've never kissed like this before. It's always been sweet, light, easy. This is raw passion, mind-blowing chemistry, a fierceness that can't be denied. This is the kind of kiss I've read in books and seen on movie screens, where two people can't get enough of each other. It's the moment they both give in, falling apart in each other's arms. I whimper as his tongue collides with mine. Neither one of us are by any means an expert kisser, but it doesn't matter. Intensity like this makes everything else dull in comparison.

We're like two sides to a coin—different, but somehow the same.

My fingers delve into his hair, knocking his beanie off in the process. He doesn't even notice. He pulls at my coat —not to take it off, but to tug me closer.

Not breaking the kiss I climb into his lap and in the same moment he slides his seat all the way back to accommodate my body on top of his. My hips sink down on his and a small, soft moan leaves my throat when I feel his erection between my legs. I wasn't expecting it and I'd be lying if I didn't say it turns me on. Finn is always so aloof and at times I've worried he's not attracted to me the way I am him, but this proves those thoughts false—although, he is a teenage boy so maybe I shouldn't get my hopes up too much.

Unable to help myself I rock my hips into him. He hisses between his teeth, but doesn't stop kissing me.

It's like a match was lit between us and now the fire is raging.

Untamable.

Unstoppable.

Unbelievable.

I take his cheeks in my hands, kissing him deeper, sinking further into him.

His hands move to my ass, gentle and soft at first, but then he growls and grips me tighter. I think it would take an out of this world force to get him to let me go.

His hips surge into mine and I gasp, the sound then sinking into a moan.

Oxygen.

I have no idea what that is at the moment. Finn is the only substantial thing in existence. He fills my lungs, surges through my veins, and heightens my senses.

I've never lost control like this before. I'm completely and utterly falling into him. I should probably be frightened by how easily I've let go, but I'm not. It feels right.

Our lips easily match the other's. We move as if we've had an entire lifetime to get acquainted.

I rock my hips into him and a soft, surprised breath stutters from his lips as they press into mine. Over and over again I roll my hips. Up. Down. Around, around. I feel something building in my body, something I've never felt before and only heard of. Sweat dampens my body beneath my heavy clothes.

"Finn," I cry out his name. "Oh my God."

My whole body shakes with an orgasm. It feels like I'm having an out of body experience. He groans into my neck, lightly biting my flesh to quiet his sounds.

A knock on the window sends us flying apart. My back hits the steering wheel and it honks.

"Knock it off. You're in public," a gruff voice grumbles from outside the steamed window.

Finn and I look at each other with wide, stunned, eyes and I let out a small laugh. Finn's eyes nervously dart from the window, back to me, but he can't do anything about his smile. His hands are still low on my hips, long fingers splayed over my butt.

"That ... that felt good."

Understatement of the century, but from Finn, it feels like I've just won an Olympic gold medal.

Somehow, I manage to get my weak legs to work and climb off his lap into the passenger seat. There's a wet spot on his jeans and color floods my cheeks, realizing we just did that in public.

Yeah, the knock on the window should've clued me in, but I was in an orgasm-induced haze.

I glance in the back, busting out in laughter when I see Jack sitting in the middle on the floor, his head cocked to the side in question.

"I don't think he's seen anything like that before," I remark.

Finn glances at Jack. "Shield your eyes next time," he chides in amusement.

"Next time?" I raise a brow, trying to hide my smile.

His smile falters a bit. "O-Only if you want to." He doesn't meet my eyes.

I reach over and grab his chin gently between my fingers, pleading for him to look at me. When he does I murmur, "I definitely want to."

I kiss him again, only briefly this time before we lose control, and buckle my seatbelt.

"G-Good," Finn stammers, putting the car in reverse. "That's good."

CHAPTER TWENTY-TWO

"You're extra smiley lately."

I look up from the food piling my plate. My mom went all out for Thanksgiving and now we have enough food to feed an army. It's way too much for only the three of us.

I try to shutter my smile, but it's impossible. It's been two days and I can't stop thinking about what happened in Finn's car. Things between us romantically have been sweet, soft, ... simple. I feared he didn't want me in that way, because he never made a move. It was silly of me, I should've expected him to be hesitant since to start he barely made conversation with me. Finn needs me to make the first move. He's too socially scarred to be forward and it's up to me to teach him, guide him, show him what my body wants and needs—and God, do I need him.

"Just happy I guess."

She smiles in return, her eyes crinkling at the corners. "It's nice to see you happy."

"Thank you." Even though I know she's being kind and truly means it, guilt settles inside me, coiling in my stomach like a slick poisonous snake. Grief, it's something that ebbs and flows, like a tide. It retreats for a time, but returns, the pit gaping open inside you once more as the pain of loss threatens to drown you. Several months ago that's all I wanted—to embrace the hurt, the despair, and let it end me, but now I'm fighting, struggling to reach the surface and breathe air fully.

"How are things going with the play?" Dad changes the subject, completely oblivious to my inner thoughts.

I turn my attention to him, swirling the gravy in my mashed potatoes, watching as the two blend together.

"It's going surprisingly well. I'm actually loving it. Mr. Rochester is a hard ass—"

"*Violet,*" my mom scolds. "That's your teacher."

"But he is, and he totally knows it," I defend, but she doesn't stop giving me the stink eye. "Mr. Rochester is very *particular,*" I decide on instead, "so he's constantly making changes and critiques, but I don't mind it because he truly makes it better."

"And what about Finn? Is he doing okay with the lead?" Worry coats her voice, and I know she's thinking of Luna and how fearful she was of such situations. To this day she has no idea about Luna trying out for the cheer team. I haven't had the heart to tell her.

"He's doing fantastic." I truly mean it too. "When he's

in character he's not Finn. He's the Beast completely. It's ... awe-inspiring."

"We can't wait to see it. Are we allowed to watch a rehearsal?"

I shake my head, chewing a bite of mac n' cheese before I answer. "Mr. Rochester has rehearsals on lockdown. He literally chewed out a janitor the other day for trying to come in and clean the auditorium. He's convinced one of the rival schools is going to steal his ideas or something, even though I'm pretty sure no one else is doing this play."

"When is the play happening?" Dad wipes his hands on a napkin and leans forward.

"Not until spring time. I think the opening is in April, but to be honest when Mr. Rochester goes on one of his dramatic rants I'm only half-listening."

"*Violet.*"

My mother again with the scolding.

I shrug innocently. "He's my favorite teacher, but he's still crazy."

She sighs heavily, but is fighting a smile so I know she's not too irritated with me.

"That's months away," my dad exclaims in disbelief.

"*Practice, practice, practice,*" I mime Mr. Rochester's tone, which he uses when one of the actors does something he doesn't approve of or forgets a line. It's usually followed by *you're a bunch of dimwitted teenagers. How did I end up subjected to this non-sense. I should've went to culinary school. God knows I would've been better than Gordon Ramsey.*

"I'm sure a play takes a lot of time to learn the lines and directions and everything," my mom interjects. "By April everything should be perfect."

I really hope she's right, because Mr. Rochester is likely to have a stroke if it's not.

"It's a big commitment," I agree, "but I don't regret doing it. I wasn't expecting the lead, but I know Mr. Rochester wouldn't give it to me if he didn't think I wasn't the best person for the role so I'm hoping I can pull it off. I'm enjoying acting way more than I ever thought I would. It started out as something to distract me, but now ... I can't explain it." I trail off, and take a couple bites of food, quiet descending over the table.

As the quiet settles, it feels heavy. My dad clears his throat and reaches over, squeezing my hand that rests on the table.

"We're proud of you, you know that, right?"

I give him a small smile. "Yeah, I know, Dad."

His eyes are sad and serious as he speaks. "I know things haven't been easy since Luna's passing, and your mom and I aren't always the best at communicating our thoughts and feelings, but we really are proud of the woman you've become. You're strong, determined, beautiful, and with the biggest heart of anyone I know. You're one in a million, Vi, don't ever let anyone make you feel any less."

"Stop getting sappy on me," I chide good-naturedly. "You're going to make me cry, and this is Thanksgiving. No tears on a holiday, it's like a rule or something."

He squeezes my hand and lets go.

We finish our meal and the three of us clean up together. Conversation is light, the heaviness gone, and I have to admit I'm enjoying the time spent with them. I was worried today would be harder than it has been, and it's made this fear settle into the pit of my stomach.

Are we getting used to Luna's absence?

Are we adjusting?

Are we only a breath away from forgetting her completely?

CHAPTER TWENTY-THREE

My phone vibrates on my bed with a text message and I roll over from the required reading I'm trying to finish—gotta love Mr. Rochester for giving an assignment over break—and am surprised when I see Finn's name on my phone. We've exchanged numbers, but haven't texted much, barely at all.

Finn: Save me.

Me: From what?

Finn: My family. They want to play charades.

Me: Lol. Can you sneak out?

Finn: I'm trapped on the couch. I'm certain my sister is acting out a dying cat. Her facial expressions are definitely something dying.

Me: Maybe she's Bambi's mom?

Finn: That's cold, Violet.

Finn: I guessed that and you were right. Not a dying cat after all, but a deer.

Me: Ooh, look at me. I'm good at this.

Finn: My brother just asked me who I'm talking to and smiling like a doofus?

Me: Oh, did he now?

Finn: I told him my girlfriend.

My breath freezes in my lungs. Air. What is air? Right, that thing I need to live, except at this moment none can be found.

Finn: Is that okay? I'll tell him I'm mistaken if you don't want to be.

Finn: Be my girlfriend that is.

Finn: Violet? Did I mess up? You know I'm no good at this stuff.

Me: You surprised me. That's all. I would love to be your girlfriend.

Finn stops replying and I worry my bottom lip between my teeth.

Finn: Yo, this is Finn's brother. I've commandeered his phone. He says you're his girlfriend and live next door. So like, if that's true, come on over.

Me: See you in a few, Husten.

Finn: Fuck, you know my name. You must be real.

I climb off my bed, tucking my phone into my jeans. I yank on some boots, grab a sweatshirt, and holler to my parents that I'm going to Finn's before I head out into the snowy cold. Thank God his house is next door. I would turn into a popsicle if it wasn't.

I reach the front door and before I can knock it swings open, two people standing there eagerly to meet me.

"You must be Husten and Della." It would be impossible for them to not be. The resemblance is uncanny. They have the same dark hair and blue eyes as Finn. Neither wears glasses, though, and Husten has a light coating of scruff on his cheeks. Della yanks me inside, wrapping her thin arms around me.

"Wow," she exhales almost dreamily, "our little Finnley has a real life, flesh and blood girlfriend. I never thought I'd see the day." When she lets me go I swear her eyes are swimming with tears. Her skin is a creamier shade than Finn's and her nose more upturned. She's beautiful, tall with a dancer's body.

"It's nice to meet you." Husten holds out a hand and I shake it. His grip is strong, and I'm sure his heavy university sweatshirt hides his bulk.

"Leave her alone," Finn pleads, appearing with Jack at his heels. He grabs for my hand and pulls me against his side.

I don't think he's aware of how he cradles me protectively against him.

"It's fine," I assure him, pressing a kiss to his smooth cheek, my left palm flat against his chest. "We're just getting to know each other."

A displeased breath passes through his lips and his siblings stand in front of us with delighted smiles.

"Do you want to join us for charades?" Della addresses

me. Her long black hair falls over her shoulders, nearly to her belly button. "Mom's already in bed, so you and Finn can be on a team, and Husten and I on the other."

Husten knocks his elbow into hers. "I don't know. Maybe we should divide the lovebirds?"

Finn takes my hand, his hold surprisingly tight and firm. "Violet is on my team. Don't even think about stealing her."

Husten raises his hands innocently and exchanges a look with Della. "Wouldn't dream of it, Finnley."

Finn and I follow his siblings down into a finished basement, complete with theatre seats and a giant screen. In the other corner there's a pinball machine and a few arcade games.

"This is cool," I remark, taking everything in.

"It's home." Della smiles as she takes a seat.

Finn and I sit down as well, and he eyes his siblings warily. I squeeze his hand in reassurance and he flashes a small hesitant smile.

"You're up first." Husten points at me.

"Me? Not fair," I grumble good-naturedly.

"How we play it here is, you have one minute to act out as many things as you can. Your partner is allowed three guesses. If they're all wrong, move on to another one. Each correct guess is a point for your team." Husten runs through the rules rapidly. "And you pick them from there." He indicates the large bowl sitting on a stool in front of the TV screen. Dramatically, he adds, "May the odds be ever in your favor."

"Thanks, Effie," I reply with a wink.

Holding my fist out to Finn he's slow to bump his against mine. "We've got this. They're going down."

He grins wholly at my game-winning attitude.

Standing, I head to the bowl and pull out a slip of paper with unfamiliar handwriting.

Can-Can Dance

I toss the piece of paper on the floor as Husten starts the timer. I begin the dance and Finn starts blabbering out words.

"Dance. Old dance?"

"One more chance," Husten interjects.

"Can-Can?" Finn's voice is puzzled but I clap and give a thumbs up, quickly grabbing another slip of paper.

Titanic (the movie)

I mime climbing up a railing and holding out my arms, a look of wonder on my face.

"Jack and Rose!" Finn shouts. I shake my head. "Titanic?"

I snap my fingers and grab another slip of paper as Husten informs us there are thirty seconds left. My heart races like I'm on a game show. My competitive side is rearing its head.

Oliver Queen

I mime shooting an arrow.

"Archer? Katniss? The Hunger Games?"

I quickly grab another.

Lord of the Rings

I mime Gollum and I'm not surprised when that's Finn's first guess.

"Lord of the Rings? The ring?"

As the time cuts off I jump and down. "Three points for us!"

I switch places with Della and Husten passes me his phone so I can keep track of the time. Once Della looks at her piece of paper I start the timer.

We go back and forth for the next hour and at the end, tally up the points.

"We won!" I cry, jumping into Finn's arms.

He's taken by surprise, rocking back, but manages to grab me and hold on.

"By one point," Husten defends. "One." He wags one finger behind Finn. "I demand a rematch before we leave Sunday.

I laugh as Finn sets me on my feet. "Whatever you want."

"You want to come back over?" Finn's surprise is palpable, and even now he can't comprehend how I like him.

"Of course." I bend down and rub Jack on top of his head. "I like hanging out with you—and you guys too," I add to his siblings who both can't stop smiling as they watch Finn and me.

"I'm just glad to see Finny is growing up," Husten jests, ruffling his brother's hair.

Finn grumbles under his breath and swats him away.

"Come on, Violet." Finn tugs me away. "I'm tired of dealing with them."

His siblings shake their heads. Finn's tone is deadpan but I also don't think he's quite serious.

He leads me upstairs and nods toward the upper level. "I ... I want to show you my room."

"Okay, lead the way."

I barely got a peek at his room months ago when I showed up to ask him to go for coffee and I'd be lying if I said I wasn't excited to get a peek at this private part of Finn's life.

He hooks his finger in mine and guides me upstairs and pauses outside his room.

"It's kind of dorky." His cheeks flush. "But it's *my* space."

He pushes the door open and my breath catches at the sight before me. There's a projector set up and stars glimmer over every surface of his bedroom. His queen-size bed is against the right wall in front of a mural of outer space, all the planets painted accurately and not in kid colors. The other walls are black chalkboard paint and Finn's drawings and handwriting cover most of the surface.

"Space, the stars, all of it—it's not just a hobby. It's my life. My future."

I spin around in awe, taking in all of the pinpoints of light marking stars.

"When it's too cold to look at the stars, I have this. It's not as good as the real thing, but it's something."

"It's beautiful."

"Come here." He tugs me down onto the big fluffy gray rug covering the wood floors.

Just like outside in the meadow, we lie down side by side and hook our pinkies together. In the corner, Jack climbs into his bed, walking in three circles before he plops.

As we lie there, Finn points out different stars, the

same ones he's shown me in the real night sky. They look different here, a little too perfect, but I can see why he loves this. It's a good substitute now that the snow keeps us from spending our nights lying in the grass together. I miss those times, especially now that things are much easier between us.

I roll over onto my side and burrow against Finn, resting my head on his chest. He stiffens in surprise at first, but then relaxes and wraps his right arm around me. He rubs my arm lazily and I feel his lips press a light kiss to my forehead.

"I like spending time with you," he murmurs, as I hook my leg around his, wiggling impossibly closer to him.

"I like spending time with you too." He has no idea how much. When I'm with Finn I feel like I'm home.

"I think you're my person, Violet."

My heart lurches in surprise at his words. I didn't expect them at all.

I raise my head slightly, staring into his eyes. He looks back, no longer afraid to make eye contact with me like he was before. He doesn't hold it for long, but the connection is enough.

"I know you're my person, Finn."

I kiss him slowly, ending it far quicker than I want to thanks to his mom and siblings being in the house. I need to go home soon, but for now, I return to my previous position and get lost in the stars projected on the ceiling, him, and hopes for a future I probably shouldn't dare dream of.

CHAPTER TWENTY-FOUR

"Thank you guys for meeting up with me," Lydia beams, her fingers wrapped around a cup of hot chocolate. My own clasp a cup of my beloved chai tea latte, courtesy of Finn.

"This should be fun. I've never ice skated before, so I'll probably fall flat on my face, but I'm excited." I watch the people already on the ice, including Husten and Della who skate like seasoned pros. Finn and I met up with Lydia at the coffee shop before walking over.

"That's your brother, right?" Lydia points, her cheeks turning pink and I'm not sure it's from the cold.

"Yeah, Husten, and my sister, Della."

Both of them wave from the ice, sensing us watching.

"I don't think I could wave and skate," I remark. "I think I'll be hugging the side the whole time."

"You don't need to do that," Finn scoffs, looking mildly offended. "I'll help you."

"Is that so?" I smile up at him, thrilled by the idea of Finn teaching me to skate.

Lydia pretends to gag. "You guys are so sweet I'm getting a stomach ache."

"We better get our skates rented." I indicate the stand and Lydia nods in agreement.

"The line was a lot longer when I pulled up to the coffee shop, so it's probably smart to get in it before there's another rush."

The three of us walk over to the line, only eight people in front of us, and make light conversation about our holiday, break, and the play.

Once we have our skates in hand we switch into them and tuck our winter boots into one of the cubbies behind the pop up stand.

I'm nervous of injuring myself, but Finn's confidence in his ability to teach me helps assuage some of my worries.

We step onto the ice and immediately my feet go out from under me. I brace for the impact of my ass colliding with the ice, but Finn grabs me, holding me up. He helps me get my balance and I grip the edge of the rink as Lydia skates past us, joining Husten and Della. I grin to myself when I see her ask Husten something.

I sense a crush stirring up.

"Hold onto my hand," Finn tells me, "and we'll skate. One foot in front of the other, slowly. Glide your foot back and forth, letting them propel you along. If you start to fall *grab* me. I've got you, Violet." With one gloved hand he cups my cheek. I'm sure they're both bright red from the frigid cold. I'm a Texas girl through and through. "I won't let you fall," he vows, his eyes serious behind his glasses. "I'm here to hold you up."

"I trust you," I whisper, and his shy smile makes butter-flies explode in my stomach.

The feeling in my chest for Finn is growing stronger every day. I'm terrified to put a word to it yet even though deep down I know what it means.

Tightening my hold on his hand—which is difficult considering our thick gloves—I let him lead me away from the side I so desperately want to stay beside.

His voice echoes in my head, telling me what to do.

"I've got you," he murmurs beside me, his voice steady and warm. His tone is encouraging and I remind myself I can do anything I set my mind to. I might need his help right now, but before we leave I'm going to skate by myself. "You're doing great," he continues, and then right on cue my feet start to lose control.

Finn's hold on me tightens and my nails claw into his down coat. I know falling isn't the biggest deal, if you fall you get back up, but I'm mostly afraid of my butt bruising and getting ice-burn. I don't know if ice-burn is actually a thing, but the idea of it is dreadful enough.

"I won't let you fall," he vows, and swings around, taking my other hand in his free one so he's skating in front of me and sort of pulling me along.

"How long have you been skating?" I figure if I ask him questions I won't worry so much about hurting myself.

"Since I was really small. It's kind of a necessity around here. You learn to walk and skate at the same time."

"Were you afraid?" I don't know why I feel the need to ask him that, it's not as if the answer is really going to make much of a difference.

He shakes his head. "I was too young to feel fear. Fear is learned. Some things are instinctual, based on survival, like knowing if you jump from too high of a height you'll die, or the way you can hold your breath but your body will force you to seek air. But when it comes to things like this, being afraid is silly. The only thing to be frightened of is yourself. Only we have the ability to hold ourselves back. We all do it, it's natural."

"How do you move past that? That ... inner block?"

He continues to skate backwards, easily thwarting our fellow skaters. I glide along with him.

"I don't know." He loosens his grip on me slightly so I'm only holding onto the edges of his fingers. "I'm still learning. I'm not sure I'll ever quite get there, but ... I'm trying. That counts for something, right?"

I smile at him and nod. "It definitely counts."

"You're helping me, you know, to get over those fears."

"I am?" I ask in surprise, my heart lurching as he lets me go even more. We're barely touching and I'm scared I'm going to fall on my face.

"Before you I wouldn't have come here. I wouldn't have dared to brave a crowd. My fear would've been it being too loud, or having a meltdown if it became too much. Growing up, when that happened, people viewed my autism as a disease they could catch. Instead of comforting me, they gave me dirty looks and told my mother to get me under control. They spoke like I couldn't hear them or understand, that I didn't have feelings. But I heard them, I knew, and those words hurt. Does anyone think I enjoy when things overwhelm me and I freak out? I wish I wouldn't react that way, but I just can't help it. Somehow, though, with you I'm learning to tune out the rest of the world. If I focus on you, on this small bubble around us, the rest of the world doesn't seem to be so much."

His words make me want to cry. I think it's the most beautiful thing anyone has ever told me, and I'm not sure anything will ever top it.

"I'm happy I can be that for you."

"Now let go," he encourages me. "Trust me to keep you safe the same way you do for me."

His words give me power and I let go. My legs wobble and my arms windmill around me, but I stay upright. Finn grins from ear to ear.

"You've got this, Violet."

I force a smile and find the power within my own body to stay upright. It's difficult, but I manage to do it.

"Move your feet. Glide," he coaches, still skating backwards in front of me. He makes it look so effortless and he's not even going *forward*.

We spend a few minutes working on my form and I grow more comfortable, not nearly as unsteady as I was before. Finn skates to my side and takes my hand so we can skate side by side. He surprises me when he kisses my cheek.

"You're doing great."

His praise lights me up from the inside.

"It's all thanks to you."

His cheeks turn a deeper shade of red not strictly from the nippy air.

Lydia has completely forgotten about us, hanging out with Husten and Della instead—well, mostly Husten. I think Finn's brother is clueless of the stars in Lydia's eyes. As a senior in college, he probably views her as a kid, but Lydia clearly thinks he's something she can take a bite from.

As Finn and I skate past them I "accidentally" knock into Lydia, sending her flying into Husten's side. They fall to the ice and he catches her in his arms.

Mission accomplished.

"You did that on purpose," Finn accuses, looking behind us at the calamity. "Why?"

"Lydia likes your brother."

He looks at me in horror. "She does? Why? I didn't notice."

"You're a boy, of course you didn't notice. She didn't tell me, but I just know. She's flipping her hair, batting her eyes, laughing at every little thing he says—she's into him, it's obvious."

"But he's my brother. He's ... gross." The look of revulsion on his face is laughable.

"To each their own." I wink at him and he looks even more confused than before. Letting go of his hand I skate a few paces and spin, all without falling. "Look, I'm doing it!" I cry triumphantly.

Pride radiates from Finn. I skate into his arms and he wraps them around me tightly.

"I don't know what this funny feeling in my chest is," he murmurs, staring down at me with warmth in his eyes, snow now falling around us, "but I like it."

I exhale a breath and we both watch the fog float through the air. Wetting my lips, I meet his eyes for a moment. "Love, Finn, I think it's love."

CHAPTER TWENTY-FIVE

"Again," Mr. Rochester demands. "Again, until you get it *perfect*."

I look at Finn, ready to cry because I'm stressed and tired, desperate to give up. The other students in the play and working behind the scenes have been gone for an hour, but Mr. Rochester won't let the two of us leave until we get this scene to match his idea of perfect—the dance between Beauty and Beast.

I understand the importance of this scene, and I want to get it right, but I'm tired. I know I have to give it my all, or we're never getting out of here.

Finn looks as tired and stressed as I am, and I think if this was any other teacher or situation he would've lost it by now, but since Mr. Rochester is the only teacher he likes he's somehow managing to keep it together.

"One more time," I tell him, holding up a finger. "We're going to nail this and get out of here."

The words sound much more confident than I feel, but I'm hoping that'll translate into how I perform.

He nods, his black curls bouncing.

We've been taking dance lessons to learn the waltz—Mr. Rochester insisted on it—and we have it pretty much nailed, but it's the *emotion* he feels we're lacking.

I'm pretty lacking in everything at the moment considering I'm starving and would love to bury my head in a bucket of KFC. I can't even remember the last time I've wanted fried chicken, but for some reason it's all I can think about.

I wonder if Finn likes KFC. Maybe we should go after—

"Reset, *now!* Do it right," Mr. Rochester demands, smacking his hand against his clipboard.

Finn and I move to the start position of entering the "ballroom" also known as the very empty stage at the moment. There are pieces of blue tape stuck to the floor to mark where we need to stand, but that's it.

I place my hand on top of Finn's and he guides me forward, spinning me around and into his arms. There is no music, but we dance anyway.

"Emote! Act with your faces!" Mr. Rochester directs from the sidelines. "This scene is all about the expressions exchanged between the characters. Show the audience what you feel."

Right now I feel like murdering you.

I don't let my thoughts show on my face, and focus on

Finn, doing my best to drown out our teacher's voice so maybe I can finally nail this.

My eyes convey to Finn that we've got this, and I know we can nail this. I have no doubt.

We dance around and around, the steps automatic now. Finn looks at me with an aching desperation and I gaze up at him with a soft expression and a slow building love. At least that's what I hope I look like.

The dance ends and Mr. Rochester claps so loudly I jump away from Finn in fear. Somehow I completely forgot that he was there, which is a miracle considering what a dictator he's been.

He hops onto the stage and smacks each of us on the back in delight. "That. *That* is what I'm looking for. Do that every time and we have a winner."

I exhale a relieved breath that somehow turns into a laugh.

"I chose you two for a reason. You have the chemistry to bring this play to life. Use that spark to your advantage. Now get out of here, I'm tired of looking at you."

Finn whistles and Jack sits up from his perch back-stage. "Let's go." He nods his head in the area of the exit and Jack trots off. Smiling at me, he tilts his head and holds out his pinky. "You too, Nebula."

Even though I'm beyond tired, I can't help the grin that splits my face as I hook my pinky around his. We walk out to the parking lot that way, the sky dark. Jack sits beside the car, waiting for us to catch up.

"I'm starving. Are you hungry?"

"You have no idea." He pushes his glasses up, his face

wrinkling in annoyance at the fact that they're always sliding down his nose. "Do you want to stop for something?"

"Please, can we? I'll text my parents and let them know."

He nods. "I'll let my mom know too."

We pile into his car, and he turns it on, letting the heat roll in. After our parents are promptly notified so they don't send out an Amber Alert, we decide to go to a local diner. It won't be KFC, but hey, beggars can't be choosers.

It only takes ten minutes to get to the mom and pop diner, parking in the side lot. Snow drifts from the sky, dusting everything, including the snow that hasn't melted on the ground from the last snowstorm.

Finn attaches Jack's leash and fixes his vest.

Inside the building, it's busier than I expected, but there are a few empty tables. I follow Finn to one in the back, tucked into a corner, and sit down. The menus are stacked on the table and I grab one. It doesn't take me long to decide to get chicken tenders. It's not exactly the fried chicken I had in mind, but it'll have to do.

We place our order and I stand up, my bladder demanding attention.

"Where are you going?" Finn blurts, his voice laced with panic that I'm abandoning him.

"I have to use the restroom. I'll be right back."

He looks around the noisy diner fearfully, like he's about to be attacked.

"I won't be long, Finn," I promise.

He nods, staring down at the table.

His reaction makes me feel horrible to leave him, but if I don't pee I'm certain my bladder is going to explode and that would be horrifically embarrassing and painful.

"Right back," I remind him, hurrying down the hall to the bathroom.

Unfortunately, *right back* proves to be a problem when there's only one bathroom and it's locked.

I rock side to side on my feet, trying to will my pee to stay cushioned in my bladder. I should've peed before we left the school, but at the time I was so desperate to get out of there I didn't think about it.

The bathroom is down a hall, so I can't see Finn. I can only hope he's doing okay.

After what feels like an eternity an elderly woman leaves the bathroom and I hurry inside. It's not the cleanest bathroom, but I have no choice, so I make quick work of peeing, careful to not let my ass touch the seat. Though, to be honest, I'm afraid that the bacteria can jump on me anyway.

I finish up and scrub my hands clean, before heading back out.

My heart freezes in my chest when I see a woman standing by the table with her hands on the shoulders of a little girl, maybe three or four years old. Finn is slumped down in the booth, his back against the wall. Jack is up in the booth, nearly on top of Finn, so I know whatever is happening is *bad.*

I run over and find the woman pointing an angry finger at Finn.

"She just wanted to pet the dog, I don't understand the

problem. You're not even supposed to have a dog in a restaurant, you know. I should call the cops on you."

"H-He's my service dog," Finn stumbles, his eyes finding me in the panic. He sags in relief, knowing I'll take care of it.

"Ma'am, what's the problem here?" I ask and she whips around, nearly hitting my face in the process with her swinging ponytail.

"The *problem*," she emphasizes, "is that my daughter tried to pet the dog and he told her *no*. She's not going to hurt it, she's just a little girl. I'd be more concerned about this mutt biting her fingers than her doing any harm."

"Well," I say as calmly as I can muster, "this is a service dog." I point to the vest that clearly labels him as such. "Which means he's working, and if someone pets him it can distract from him doing his job. All of his focus needs to be on Finn so he can help if he needs to."

The woman looks back at Finn. "You don't look sick. Nothing's wrong with you. Those are meant for people who are sick, or missing limbs or something. Not normal teenagers."

"*Ma'am*," my tone grows tight, "you need to back away."

She whips back to me. "Not until my daughter gets to pet the dog."

Everyone in the diner is looking at us now, but not doing anything to help. I guess it's easier to sit back than it is to stand up and make noise.

"Are you crazy?" I blurt. "I just told you this is a service dog. You *can't* pet him and neither can *she*." I point at her little girl. Irritation is getting to me and my patience is wearing thin.

The owner chooses that moment to appear from the back. "What's the problem here?"

I butt in before the uneducated swine in front of me can utter a word. "This woman here, thinks she's entitled to pet my boyfriend's *service* dog. That's not how this works."

The owner, a man who appears to be in his fifties or so, turns to her and begins explaining everything I've already said. She huffs, rolls her eyes, and finally storms out the door dragging her daughter with her.

"Your meal is on me," the owner tells me. "I'm terribly sorry—"

He's cut off when Finn suddenly bolts out of the booth, his hold on Jack's leash tight. He doesn't make eye contact with me as he passes, instead his head is down, his shoulder drawn upwards like he's trying to disappear into himself.

"Finn." He ignores me so I run after him and outside into the cold. "*Finn.*"

He doesn't stop, he unlocks his car, letting Jack jump inside.

"Finn, what's wrong?" I plead, panicking now. He's completely shut down, and reminds me of the closed off boy I first got to know. He gets behind the driver's seat and closes the door. I don't even have a chance to get to the passenger side before he's backing out at too fast of a speed, completely ignoring my pleas and the tears now streaming down my cheeks.

I feel the tether between us fraying, slipping from my grasp. The rope I've slowly been tugging to bring us closer is being let go by him and I'm coming crashing back down to Earth, to reality, when all I want is to be lost in the stars with him.

His brake lights flash in the dark before he turns out of the lot.

The reflection of the red taillights on the snow reminds me of blood.

It feels significant somehow, like it's the life of our relationship bleeding out.

I stand there for too long, until I'm shivering, lips quivering, with my fingers turning a bruised shade of blue. I dig my phone out of my pocket and make a call.

"M-Mom? I need you to come get me."

CHAPTER TWENTY-SIX

I'VE NEVER BEEN IN LOVE BEFORE, EXPERIENCED THE death of a relationship. The raw, gutting feeling of having a knife carve out your feelings. My emotions feel ripped open and devastation sits heavy in my chest like the weight of an elephant.

I don't know what I did, how this was my fault, but it feels like it is.

It's been weeks and Finn hasn't spoken a word to me, beyond running our lines for the play. Somehow, he manages to face me for that, but disappears before I can corner him behind the stage. He no longer visits the auditorium for lunch and I haven't found him hiding elsewhere in the school, though I suspect he's going to his car.

I returned home that night from the diner after my mom came to pick me up. I cried the whole way home, knowing in my gut Finn and I were over, but seeing my stuff sitting in a neat pile under the cover of the front porch was my undoing.

My mom guided me up to bed and held me as I cried, running her fingers through my hair like she used to when I was a little girl and would get hurt doing something silly.

But I would take that physical pain over this devastation and feeling like my heart has been carved in two. This isn't even a clean cut. No, it's jagged, with rough edges and gashes.

I know the woman's actions had to be upsetting for him, but I wish I knew what *I* did that's driven him away. I was trying to help and it seems I failed epically at it.

Lydia slides down the wall beside me, a paper bag containing her lunch—chicken salad sandwich, apple, and one mini Reese cup if the rest of the week is any indicator.

"You're the saddest sap I've ever seen," she remarks, digging into the bag and pulling out the green apple.

I don't like green apples. I prefer red, but to each their own, I guess.

She takes a bite.

Crunch, crunch, crunch.

"Next week is Christmas break, you shouldn't be so sad. The holidays are no time to be sour, at least according to my mother."

I sigh, eyeing my own packed lunch. I've barely touched it.

Despite the fact I keep finding different halls to eat my lunch in, Lydia always seeks me out. I tell myself I'm hiding from her, but I'm always secretly glad when she does find me and I'm not alone. She's not a bad person, I actually really like her, but she's not Finn.

"He misses you," she whispers softly under her breath.

I let out a humorless laugh. "No, he doesn't."

"I see it in the way he looks at you."

I shake my head. "He doesn't look at me."

"He does, but only when he knows you won't catch him."

"I really don't want to talk about Finn." My tone is pleading, begging her to let it go.

"Okay, what *do* you want to talk about?" She takes another bite of her apple, chewing and giving me a minute to think.

"Nothing."

She makes a buzzing noise. "Wrong answer."

I sigh heavily. "What's the right answer then?"

"Mr. Rochester and his dicktator ways—that's dictator with a k by the way." I snort, because she's not wrong. "The play. Break. Prom. Graduation. The future. There are lots of things to talk about that don't involve the dreaded F word."

"Maybe I'm just not in the mood to talk."

"Fair enough." She shrugs, leaning her back against the wall.

A few minutes pass and I can't help but ask her a question. "Still talking to Husten?"

Her cheeks color. "A little bit."

I bump her shoulder with a genuine smile. "Get it, girl!" I do a little shimmy and she smiles shyly.

"I doubt it'll go anywhere. I mean, he's graduating

college soon and I'm going to be starting college in the fall. I must be a kid to him."

I roll my eyes. "Lydia, if he thought you were a kid he wouldn't have given you his number."

She assesses my words. "That's true." A wistful smile touches her lips. "Who knows where it will go, then."

I pick a grape from the baggy positioned precariously on my leg and pop it in my mouth. I don't want to eat, but I know I have to. I find when I'm sad I don't have an appetite. After Luna's death it felt like I didn't eat for a solid month. I know that's not true, but I could barely stomach anything and ate very little.

The fact that I can see Finn, speak to him, but he's not mine, not anymore, is painful. Losing Luna, and the boy I've fallen for, all in less than a year feels like some sort of cruel Greek tragedy.

Maybe that's my teen melodramatics coming out, but I think losing Luna has left me raw and vulnerable in ways and places I'm only beginning to fathom, and having Finn walk away from me has exposed them.

"It's okay to be sad, you know." Lydia's stare cuts through me. "You don't have to keep it all inside."

"It's easier that way." I grab another grape, roll it around in my fingers, before tossing it like a mini-basketball in the trash can across the way. It bounces off the lip and rolls away down the hall and out of sight.

"Well, I'm here if you need me."

She wads up her now empty paper bag, stands and brushes her butt free of dust and debris on the school floor, and throws her trash away before, just like the grape, she's gone.

———

FINN STANDS two feet in front of me.

In reality he's *right* there. I can touch him. See him. Smell him. *Feel* him.

But he's not mine.

He runs his lines and mine leave my mouth on autopilot. I know the play backwards and forwards now, especially with us not talking. It's all I really have to focus on.

As much as I try to suppress my thoughts when we're rehearsing, it's more difficult at times. Today, I want nothing more than to beat his chest with my fists, begging for him to explain what I did, why he left me just like Luna did.

I guess that's the root of my problem, though.

I've never admitted to anyone, not even myself, how betrayed I've felt by Luna's suicide. She *abandoned* me to live in a world without her, when she was one of the best things in it. Finn helped fill that void, not completely, but there wasn't a black hole inside me anymore threatening to swallow me. It isn't because Finn's autistic like she was, though some might would think that's the reason, it's just *him*. There's something in his being, his DNA, that calls to me. It's unexplainable, and having him act like we're strangers is killing me.

I don't know how he manages to recite his lines and

perform as if nothing is wrong between us when every-thing is.

"Excellent!" Mr. Rochester's voice booms from below where he sits in the front row, his trusty clipboard for notes perched on his knee. "Let's move on to the scene of Beast in the bathtub."

Finn turns away from me, ready to begin his next scene, and with a hefty exhale I bleed away and exit stage right. I find a place to sit on the stairs, out of sight and in the semi-dark. Resting my head against the wall I try to control my emotions, but it's useless, and soon tears are falling down my face. I brush them away as fast as I can, but they keep coming.

I feel pathetic crying over a boy, but I guess that's the thing, I'm not just crying over him. It's him, it's Luna, it's moving here, it's saying goodbye to the person I used to be.

"Whatever happens, you'll get through this," I whisper to myself, gripping the stair railing in my right hand and pulling myself up.

Turning around, I wipe my wet cheeks with the backs of my hands. Thank God I wore waterproof mascara or it would be smeared all the way down my face by now.

A small gasp passes through my lips when I see Finn standing at the top of the stairs.

His eyes meet mine for the briefest of seconds, and before he can run away from me, I blurt, "You broke my heart."

His head bows, shoulders drawn, and for a second I think I see shame spread over his face.

Then, like always, he's gone.

CHAPTER TWENTY-SEVEN

"Merry Christmas!" The cries from my parents scare me, and I jump back, banging the heel of my foot into the bottom stair. The pain stings all the way up my leg, but I don't let it show.

"Merry Christmas." My response is soft, reserved.

I don't feel much like celebrating.

It has nothing to do with Finn and everything to do with Luna.

She loved Christmas. If she were here, she'd be dressed in holiday pajamas and dragged me out of bed long before now. Usually she woke up around five in the morning on Christmas. I used to gripe about it. I wouldn't now.

I guess that's what hindsight is for, to show us that sometimes things we might find irritating are actually moments of comfort. If you change your view of things, it changes your whole outlook on how you feel.

I don't want my sadness to put a damper on today, so I force a smile on my face and follow them into the family room. Over night gifts have appeared under the tree.

I wonder if any are from Santa this year. Even though I stopped believing long ago, Luna hadn't, so there were always presents from Santa. I hope there are, it'll feel like Luna is here in some small way.

"Do you want to start opening them?" My mom asks with a hopeful smile.

"Or eat first?" My dad interjects. "We'll do whatever you want."

We always used to open presents first. The excitement overrode hunger.

"Presents," I reply, and this time when I smile it's genuine.

I know my parents are doing the best they can. They're hurting too, but they're trying to be strong for me.

I find an empty spot on the floor to sit and they join me, passing me gifts they want me to unwrap in a certain order. It's mostly clothes, but I also get a new music speaker and hair straightener. My mom passes me the last present and my heart lurches when I see *To Violet, From Santa*.

I unwrap it, finding a book on the solar system.

My mom reaches out, tucking a piece of dark hair behind my ear. "I know Finn isn't talking to you now, but he will, I know it, and in the meantime I thought you could learn more about what he loves."

"Thanks, Mom." I swallow past the lump in my throat and reach out, wrapping an arm around her shoulders. "I mean, Santa." A small giggle bubbles out of my throat. I don't know how she knows about this, but mom's just seem to have that magical ability.

"I still think you should let me give him a piece of my mind," my dad grumbles. "Leaving you like that in the snow wasn't nice of him."

I shake my head and smile at my dad. "That's not necessary."

He mutters something under his breath that sounds suspiciously like *all boys are idiots*.

"I have a present for you guys," I announce, and hop up. "Let me grab it."

I run upstairs and dig out the small box from my dresser. I used every dollar I've saved for years doing odd jobs, plus stooped to asking my grandparents for help covering the rest. But I wanted to do something special for my parents, and since I opted to be in the play that meant not getting a job to have spending money.

I hurry down the stairs, truly feeling elated to give them their gift.

"Open it together." I hold out the slender box, the size one might find a necklace in, wrapped in paper with cheerful snowmen on it. "Grams and Papaw helped me, but..." I trail off, giving a small shrug.

They rip off the paper and open the lid.

Their jaws drop as they look at each other and then swing their gazes to me with twin expressions of surprise.

"I bought the tickets. Grams and Papaw paid for the hotel costs."

"Vi," my mom breathes, placing her hand over her mouth. "I ... wow. I don't know what to say."

I shrug like it's no big deal, because it's not, not to me anyway. They deserve this after everything. A chance to get away, just the two of them.

She clutches the plane tickets to Seattle to her chest and tears fall down her cheeks. My dad still hasn't said a word. I think from his expression he's in shock, but confused as well.

"You guys have always talked about going to Seattle," I chatter to fill the silence. "Now you can."

My mom pulls me into a bone-crushing hug. "Violet, my beautiful, thoughtful, one-of-a-kind, daughter—you are the best parts of me and your father. Don't ever doubt how bright your soul shines and the kindness in your heart. Everyone can see it, feel it."

She lets me go and my dad, finally able to function, hugs me as well.

"I love you, Vi." He kisses the side of my forehead.

"Love you, too, Dad." I squeeze him in a hug.

My mom wipes her tears away, stands, and begins to gather the trash up.

I help and my dad heads into the kitchen to start on breakfast. Every Christmas he makes his "world famous" crepes. I don't tell him that I'm pretty sure only *he* thinks they're famous and the French would probably be ashamed to see what he calls crepes. I always eat them with the biggest smile, though.

She ties the full trash bag and holds it out to me. "Mind running this out to the cans?"

"Not a problem." I take it from her, and since it's full of mostly wrapping paper it's not too heavy.

Sliding my feet into my slippers I open the garage door and head out into the cold. I don't bother with a coat, which is probably dumb, but I only need to dispose of the bag in the can beside the house.

I round the house and noise startles me. Dropping the bag I turn around and spot Finn walking out of the side of his house, like me carrying a trash bag.

My heart pitter patters a wild beat and I silently tell it to cut it out, that it has to stop feeling this way for Finn, but of course it doesn't listen. It never does. Hearts are wild loose cannons we have no control over.

Finn pauses beside the trashcan. He doesn't quite look at me, but he isn't not looking either. Despite my lack of outerwear I'm hot all over. I'm surprised the snow isn't melting beneath my feet.

The moment stretches out and I watch him closely.

His ticks.

The way his fingers on his left hand tap against his thigh. How his right hand tightens around the white plastic bag. The wiggle of his nose as he tries to stop his glasses from sliding down. His lips twitch the slightest bit like he wants to say something, but thinks he shouldn't.

Finally, he murmurs, "Merry Christmas," opens the trashcan and shoves the bag in it before hurrying back inside.

I swallow past the lump in my throat. "Merry Christmas, Finn."

I pick up the trash, throw it away, and paste a smile on my face as I go back in the house.

It's easier to pretend, than to admit to myself that I'm breaking all over again.

CHAPTER TWENTY-EIGHT

New Year's Eve.

The day we say goodbye to one year and hello to another. It's a chapter closed, another opened. It's a fresh page in a new book. A blank slate.

Three-hundred and sixty-five days to create a whole new you.

Few of us ever actually accomplish that feat, even if we try.

As much as we like the idea of becoming *new*, there's no such thing. We might change and grow through the years, but we keep pieces of our past selves with our new selves.

There's a lot from this past year that I know I'll carry over into the next—probably for the rest of my life. There's something about the loss of a loved one that changes our fundamental beings. First love changes us too. I've been so wrapped up in how I felt with Finn, the high of falling in love with him, that I didn't consider first loves don't always equal lasts.

Not speaking to him sucks.

Not seeing my sister every day sucks.

Not understanding what I did wrong with Finn sucks.

Not being able to go back and change things so my sister is still alive *sucks*.

So much suckage, and yet life moves on and you either have to move with it or get mowed over.

It's a little bit above freezing, but it doesn't stop me from bundling up and sitting on the roof outside my bedroom window. If my mom saw me she'd either yell at me about catching a cold or be afraid I might fall.

I won't fall. I don't want to. I want to fly instead.

The sky is dark and I hear fireworks in the distance, ringing in midnight.

January first.

The start of something new, but a continuation all the same.

Some of the fireworks are high enough for me to see them barely peek over the tops of the trees. I lean back, watching them, ignoring the cold searing my ass through my sweatpants.

I feel eyes on me and I know, know instinctively deep in my soul, that Finn is watching me. I don't look for his eyes in the dark. It'll hurt too much when he finds me looking and invariably runs from me, even though I'm on the roof and hardly in a position to corner him easily.

I wonder what he sees when he looks at me.

Only he knows why he won't talk to me.

I keep replaying the night in the diner over and over, trying to think about my actions and words, how anything I said or did might've scared him.

I'm coming up empty, but the fact remains, something did happen.

I stay outside on the roof until the fireworks end. It can't be more than five minutes. Before I crawl back in, my eye catches Finn's tall form by the backdoor of his house. He's leaning against the siding like he's trying to blend in.

It wasn't too long ago when we were meeting every night in the field behind our homes, finding solace in the stars and solar system above us. It feels like a lifetime ago.

I inhale a shaky breath and let it out, my breath fogging the night air.

"I'm sorry," I murmur.

I know he can't hear my apology, but I hope he feels it.

CHAPTER TWENTY-NINE

School starts up and it's back to the regular grind immediately, and before I know it, it's the middle of January.

With senior year months away from coming to a close, most classes are beyond boring with basically no work. Except Mr. Rochester's of course. I appreciate having to put hard work in. The rest of the classes are now boring and seem like a pointless waste of time.

I walk the halls, waiting for them to clear until I have to head to the auditorium for practice. The sets and costumes are almost completely done, but even with all the behind the scenes stuff shaping up nicely, there's still work to be done on performances.

Mainly, mine.

My heart isn't in like it was, and while I was initially

good at faking my scenes with Finn, it's acting after all, now my irritation and sadness is bleeding into it. Anger too. Some days I just want to smack my fists against Finn's chest to get out my frustrations with him. I never do, and I wouldn't, so instead I've taken to walking the halls as they empty out for the day. There's something peaceful about seeing the school empty of bodies at the end of the day, the calm and quiet that settles over the normally raucous halls.

I trail my fingers against the walls.

"Page!" I jump at the sound of my name being yelled behind me. I turn around rapidly. Mr. Rochester stands at the end of the hall. "Auditorium is that way."

"I know. I was just walking."

His eyes narrow. "What's wrong with you? You've been different lately."

He walks down the hall, closing the distance between us. His brows are narrowed, but his eyes are concerned.

"You've got me worried, Violet." He pauses in front of me, tipping his head to the side.

I shrug. "It's nothing important. Typical teenage angst."

He harrumphs. "I might believe that with other kids, not you. You don't want to talk about it, that's fine, but I'm here if you ever need to talk." He lifts a finger in warning. "Just don't tell anyone I said that. I don't want to listen to the rest of these fuckers blabber about their petty problems."

I let out a small, genuine laugh. "It's a secret."

"I have to grab stuff from my classroom and then I'll be there. Don't be late."

"I won't."

He heads one way and I go the other, hands shoved in my pockets. I walk a little faster, knowing there will be hell to pay if Mr. Rochester beats me to the auditorium.

Opening the heavy doors, I walk down the aisle and backstage. I pass by Finn sitting on the floor looking at a script with Jack beside him.

He raises his head, but I don't acknowledge him in any way. Clearly he's not going to talk to me, and I need to just let it go and move on, so that means doing my best to pretend he's not there.

That he doesn't affect me.

It's easier said than done.

I find Lydia on the opposite side, working on a costume for Mrs. Potts, a pin stuck between her teeth.

I pull out a stool and sit down beside her. "Already getting to work I see." I crack a smile at her as she focus on placing the pin.

"Figured I might as well before the tyrant arrives." She sticks out her tongue.

"I heard that." Mr. Rochester's shoes thump against the stairs up to backstage. Papers are clasped in his right hand and he bypasses us, heading over to the student, Jacob, playing Lumiere.

We can't hear what he says, but from the way he hands Jacob the papers and begins gesturing madly I assume it's notes on what he thinks needs to be approved on for the role.

"I honestly don't know why he doesn't direct plays for

an actual theater," Lydia grumbles, glancing over at him, "instead of torturing us."

The girl playing Mrs. Potts, Samantha, snorts. "It's because no one would put up with his shit. We have no choice."

"Except to quit," I point out.

Her eyes drop to me. "Trust me, no one would dare. I heard once that a kid dropped a week before opening night because of the pressure and Mr. Rochester showed up at his house and forced him to go do the play."

"That sounds like a really exaggerated rumor to me."

But also, I wouldn't put it past him.

She narrows her eyes on me. "That's what I *heard*."

"Then obviously it *must* be true," I snap sarcastically.

"No wonder you have no friends," she sneers. "You're rude as hell. *Ow!*" She glowers at Lydia. "That hurt."

Lydia holds up a pin. "Oops. Sorry."

Her tone and grin tells me she's not sorry at all.

She doesn't know, but Samantha's words don't bother me. The majority of the school ignores me and those who don't give me weird looks.

For all the time I've spent with Finn.

For keeping to myself.

For ... God knows what.

I'm learning teenagers can dislike someone for the pettiest of reasons and it's too exhausting to even bother trying to fathom what they are.

Mr. Rochester claps his hands and calls for the cast to join him.

Samantha tears away from Lydia, ripping a piece of her dress in the process.

Lydia gasps, looking ready to cry at the big gap in the ending sequence dress she's been constructing.

"Oh, did I do that?" Samantha asks, knowing very well she did. "Guess you'll just have to fix it."

Lydia grumbles under her breath, "Or you could not be a bitch."

"Excuse me?" Samantha raises a brow.

Lydia smiles up at her. "I didn't say a thing."

I give Lydia's shoulder a reassuring squeeze before I stand up and join the cast around Mr. Rochester.

Once we're all there he begins.

"Opening night is officially April first. It's earlier than I expected and *no*, Mr. Collins," he growls when a student raises a hand, "this is not an April Fool's Day prank, though I wish it was." Clearing his throat, he peers around at us, making eye contact with everyone. "This means we're going to have to work even harder to be ready in time for opening night. I expect you all to work one-hundred and ten percent when you're here. We need this to be perfect." He slams the bottom of his fist against the palm of his opposite hand.

Finn slowly raises his hand. He *never* speaks out in a large group setting like this, so to see him do so willingly is shocking to me.

Even Mr. Rochester is surprised. "Uh, yes Mr. Crawford? What is it?"

"You said we have to give one-hundred and ten

percent, but there's no such thing. It's one-hundred percent or less, there's nothing above."

Mr. Rochester cracks a smile. "Indeed you're right, Mr. Crawford. It's an exaggeration to get the point across of how hard I need you all to work at this."

"But..." Finn pauses, his eyes dropping to his shoes. He toes them against the wooden floor. "We can't work harder than a hundred percent."

Mr. Rochester's lips quirk with the threat of a smile. "All right, give *one-hundred* percent on this. I'm believing in you all, trusting you to bring this to life. Do not disappoint me. I don't accept failure." He looks around at all of us once more, assessing the group, and then nods to himself. "Now, let's get to work. We have two and a half months to get this *perfect*."

CHAPTER THIRTY

"Be my Valentine?" Someone slides into the seat beside me.

I grin and accept the red heart-shaped lollipop Lydia offers me. I don't know how she manages to find me, today I'm hiding out in the library during my free period.

"Of course." I pull out the small box of chocolates from my purse and give them to her. "Only if you'll be mine?"

She takes the box and opens them. "Ooh, caramel chocolates. I'll definitely be your Valentine."

"What about Husten, though?" I probe. "I'm not much for sharing."

She sticks her tongue out. "There's enough of me to go around, don't be jealous." Her cheeks coloring she whispers, "He sent a dozen roses to my house and my mom nearly had a heart attack. She's now planning our wedding." She shakes her head. "I think that woman would rather have me married straight out of high school and start giving her grandchildren than see me go off to college."

"Ugh, college," I groan, dread filling my tone.

I didn't apply for early admission anywhere like my dad wanted, but I did manage to get applications out regardless.

"You don't want to go?" she asks, sounding genuinely confused.

"No, I do," I sigh. "I just ... I feel too young to be making that kind of decision."

"Yeah, I know what you mean." She nods along as we watch students pass in front of us. "I guess we just have to see where things lead us."

My heart lurches. "It's that lack of control that scares me the most."

She gives a soft laugh. "Violet, when it comes to life, there is no such thing as control."

The bell rings and my body fills with dread that I have to head off to Physics. I have the stupid class every day and it's my least favorite one. It wasn't so bad when I was talking to Finn, but now that he ignores me it's the worst fifty minutes of my life and I have to repeat it five days a week.

I stand and sling my backpack over my shoulders, gathering my papers in my arms and the lollipop from Lydia.

"See you later," I tell her as we head our separate ways.

I barely make it into the classroom before the bell rings and I hurry to my spot beside Finn. He's already there, head propped on his hand, looking directly at the black tabletop so he can ignore my presence.

Jack's head lifts from the ground as I sit down and he gives me a sad look.

I miss you too, buddy.

Mr. Lambert closes the door to the classroom and gets straight to today's lesson.

I wish it was easier to pay attention to him, but my body is always hyper aware of Finn. My arms tingle with his nearness and I yearn to look at him, but I don't. I can't. He's not mine anymore, not my boyfriend, and not even my friend.

I ruined everything and I don't even know how.

That's the most frustrating part.

But because I care about Finn, I'm doing my best to let it go. I know if I bugged him about it, it would be nothing but upsetting for him, and he doesn't deserve that.

Even with this, I still care about how he feels.

Maybe that makes me pathetic, but I think that's how love works. Sacrificing your own happiness for someone else.

When the fifty minutes is up I stand to gather my stuff. Normally, Finn runs away as quickly as he can, but instead he pauses and bends down, adjusting something on Jack's collar.

I look away, shuffling my papers on the desk into a neat pile before picking my backpack up off the floor.

"Happy Valentine's day, Finn," I whisper, making the briefest of eye contact with him—on his part, not mine, because *God* does it hurt to look at him.

He doesn't say anything back, but I feel his eyes on me as I leave the room.

———

I ARRIVE HOME FROM SCHOOL, exhausted from rehearsals, and ready to fall apart.

I toss my backpack on my bed and get Will Ferret from his cage, cuddling him to my chest.

"Hey, buddy, I missed you." I kiss the soft top of his head as I close the blinds in my room. If they're closed I can't be tempted to look next door.

I let Will run around while I shower in my attached bathroom and change into my PJs.

My damp hair hangs around my shoulders and I open my backpack to switch out my books for the ones I'll need tomorrow.

A small Valentine's card like the ones we used to get in elementary school falls out, dropping to the floor, and I bend down to pick it up.

I open it and my heart stops.

It's covered in yellow stars, with a rocket ship, and those interconnecting lines that form constellations.

You're out of this world, it says.

On the back, it says *to Nebula from Finn*.

I look toward my closed blinds, knowing on the other side, across the way, is Finn.

Maybe it's dumb, but the silly valentine gives me hope.

I hold it against my chest and close my eyes.

CHAPTER THIRTY-ONE

"Seriously, you have to stop pining. You're making me all kinds of sad and shit. It's not cool," Lydia jokes, though I'm sure it's not a complete joke, as she works on perfecting my yellow ball gown for the dance sequence. "Just talk to him."

"It's not that simple," I mutter under my breath, forcing my eyes away from Finn about six feet away while another student works on his costume.

"Boys are infuriating," she agrees. "That's why I like Husten. He's a man."

I laugh at that. "Do boys ever really become men, or are they just older boys?"

She sticks her tongue out at me. "You have a point. Now turn." She swirls her finger in the air and I swivel around in the heavy dress. Finn and I have the dance number nailed *but* dancing in this dress will be a definite challenge. It's huge.

"He misses you, you know. I see it in the way he looks at you."

I snort. "Finn never looks at me anymore. It's like I'm a blank wall he can easily pass by."

She shrugs. "Maybe you're not looking when he is, because believe me, I catch him taking peeks at you all the time."

I want to believe her, and she has no reason to lie, but I don't want to get my hopes up. It's nearly March and he hasn't spoken to me since the incident at the diner, beyond telling me to leave him alone and the brief encounter Christmas day.

Out on the main stage Mr. Rochester works with other cast members and I listen to what he's saying because it helps me to better ignore Finn.

Lydia continues to work for a while until finally directing me to get down off the short platform I was standing on. She guides me to a mirror and I gasp as I look at my reflection in the mirror. I might look a mess, my dark hair barely tamed and my eyes tired, but the dress is stunning. It's a work of art.

"Lydia, it's a crying shame if you don't go into the fashion industry. This is incredible."

Her cheeks turn pink in her reflection behind me. "Thank you." She pulls a loose thread on the sleeve.

I then change out of the dress and back to my regular clothes and prepare to run through the scene where Belle begs Beast to live.

It's also the scene where I'm to kiss Finn.

We've never practiced the kiss, but today that changes.

It shouldn't bother me, I've kissed him after all, but this feels wrong.

I meet Finn on the stage and find him tugging on the sleeves of his shirt. They're already down to his wrists but he keeps trying to pull them further down. I can feel his frustration vibrating from his body several feet away from him. I don't know what to do to help him, and I doubt he'd want my help anyway.

"Okay, you two," Mr. Rochester marches over, "we're going to run through the full scene. Start to finish. I'm going to..." He closes his eyes and takes a steadying breath. "Do my best not to comment or critique. I want to see how you guys perform." He takes another moment to gather himself. "We're going to start with Beast on the ground after he's been shot by Gaston. You're going to run to him, Violet, and—"

"Mr. Rochester," I interrupt before he can go on a tangent. "We've got this. Trust us."

He pinches his brow. "Don't disappoint me you two."

He climbs off the stage and takes his place in a seat in the front row.

Finn and I go to our designated places. Taking a deep breath I steady myself and close my eyes as I allow myself to transform into Belle. It might sound dramatic, but I find the process of essentially stepping into her character in my mind to work the best for me. It allows me to *become* her and not just recite lines by heart. I feel everything she would feel if she were real.

I hear Mr. Rochester tell us to begin and I leave Violet behind.

That's not Finn. It's Beast, and he's hurt.

I run over, falling to my knees.

My lines roll out of my lips and I cup his cheeks in my hands. His eyes are closed in feigned death and I let the tears come to my eyes, spilling over.

"I love you," I whisper. "Come back to me. I love you, do you hear me? I love *you*." I lower my head and press my lips to his softly. Mine are pillowed against his and he doesn't move. He's not supposed to, not yet anyway.

But then he does.

His fingers curl into my long hair at the nape of my neck and his lips begin to move. He kisses me back deeply, his tongue finding the seam of my lips. I open for him and suddenly I know he's not the Beast anymore.

He's Finn.

I'm Violet.

And we're not acting.

I can't hear the voices of the others, nothing else exists at all. It's just the two of us. Even the past few months flee my mind as he kisses me. It feels so right.

I don't know how long passes until we break apart. I stare down at him in surprise. His blue eyes are so dark they're nearly black. His fingers stay clasping my hair and his eyes dip to my swollen lips.

"Whoa," someone says behind us.

I jump away from Finn, brought abruptly back to reality as I realize we're not alone.

My heart races in my chest and my cheeks redden with

embarrassment at making out in front of the entire theatre production.

"I-I have to go," I stutter, turning sharply on my heel and running away.

My feet slam against the steps as I run down them. I feel eyes watching me as I sprint up the aisle and out the large doors into the center of school. I keep running outside, letting the main doors slam closed behind me.

I bend over then, hands on my knees, as tears choke me.

Why does this hurt so much?

I cry for me, for Finn, for Luna, for every single thing. I let the pain bleed out of me.

The doors close sharply again and I whip around coming face to face with Finn. His dark floppy hair is blown back from his forehead and his chest rises and falls sharply with each breath.

"You ran after me?" I accuse, wiping frantically at my wet face. "Why?" I take a step forward, my tone harsh. "Why, when you *left* me? You left me just like Luna did. You both had a *choice* and you still left me anyway!" I shout at him, my voice raw and anguished.

I guess that's the root of my problem.

I'm so Goddamn angry.

At Luna for choosing to take her life.

At my parents for running away.

At Finn for leaving me.

At myself.

Mostly at myself, because I feel like I should've done

more, been more, for the people around me and no matter how hard I try it's not good enough.

"Nebula—"

"No!" I hold up a hand. "You don't get to choose to talk to me now. Not when I've been trying so hard for *months*. You broke my heart, Finn. Don't think you can just hold it together for a few seconds with pretty words and everything will be all right. It doesn't work like that."

He glances down, but not before I see the hurt flash across his face.

"I wasn't good enough for Luna to stay, and I'm not good enough for you either," I sob, clutching my chest as I struggle to get enough air into my aching lungs. Spreading my arms to my sides I continue, "All I have to offer is me, and clearly that doesn't cut it."

He opens his mouth again but I shake my head, cutting him off. "Just don't."

I turn and walk away.

Maybe I'm being dramatic. I'm only seventeen after all, but I'm exhausted. Giving my heart to people isn't easy, and constantly having it torn apart is killing me. Enough is enough.

Sometimes we have to choose ourselves over others, and that's what I'm doing.

CHAPTER THIRTY-TWO

I STIR MY CEREAL AROUND AND AROUND. LIFTING THE spoon I watch the milk spill off of it and back into the bowl.

"I want to see a therapist," I announce.

My parents both look up rapidly from their own bowls of cereal and my dad sets his iPad down where he was reading the paper on an app.

After Luna's suicide my parents broached the idea of me going to a therapist but I turned them down. They went to a few sessions on their own, but I wanted no parts of it. It felt like failure to me to admit I needed help in that way. Now, I wish I had.

"All right, I'll see if I can get you in with someone."

I'm surprised by mom's ready agreement. Not that I thought either of them would say no, but I did expect a lot of questions.

Like, *why now?* Or, *did something happen?*

"Thank you," I quietly murmur the words into my cereal bowl like it's the one that's going to make my appointment.

I'm not sure therapy will solve all my problems, the hurt and anger I'm only beginning to realize I've held onto so tightly, but it seems like a good start.

I feel my parents exchange a look rather than see it. I don't want to worry them, but I know deep down this is something I need to do in order to heal. Luna's death will always be a part of me, but the anger doesn't have to be forever.

———

My mom is able to get me in with a therapist two weeks later.

The office is surprisingly warm, and not the sterile cold thing I expected. It's painted a soft brown color and instead of the standard waiting room chairs there are several comfortable couches. My mom sits beside me, clutching her purse in her lap. She looks more nervous than me.

I wait for my name to be called and when it is I give her a reassuring smile before I stand, smoothing my hands down my jeans, and head back.

"I'm Dr. Lee." The cheery dark-skinned woman in her forties greets me. "Take a seat wherever you'd like."

Inside the room there's a couch and two chairs.

I choose the couch.

She takes a chair.

I notice she doesn't have a notebook or anything of the sort.

It's just me and her, having a conversation. Or about to, anyway.

"I'm glad you're here today, Violet."

I nod, tucking a piece of hair behind my ear as I look around.

There's no desk. Or awards. Or plaques. It's just a simple room with a window overlooking the shopping center across the street, framed photos of buildings downtown on the walls, and bookshelves with everything from children's books to non-fiction.

"How much do you know?" I ask her, probing to see what my mom might've told her when making my appointment.

She crosses her legs. "Nothing. I like to keep it that way. I want you to trust me, and since you don't know me it's only fair I don't know you either."

I give a small smile.

"What's your favorite color?" I ask her. I know it's her job to get to know me, but I'm not ready just yet. I need to get comfortable.

"Red." I bet it's the shade of the color lipstick she wears that she likes so much.

I brush the backs of my fingers against my jeans like I'm flicking away crumbs, but really I'm just buying time.

She's a therapist, so I'm sure she knows that.

"My sister killed herself." The words are uttered

quietly, like I don't want to give them voice to this stranger. "T-That's why I'm here."

She tilts her head, but her expression doesn't change.

I don't know if putting it out there like that is what I'm supposed to do, but it seems like a waste of therapy not to get straight to the point.

"She was younger than me." I look out the window. "Too young to make that decision."

"Why do you say that?"

I snort. "A middle school kid taking their own life is too young. She had her whole life ahead of her. One where it could get better. But she chose to leave instead."

Dr. Lee is quiet for a moment. "Maybe she thought it would never get better. Maybe she didn't see any other option."

I wince and face Dr. Lee head on. "She could've come to me. Talked to me. To our mom. Our dad. She didn't."

"Maybe she did in her own way."

"Are you playing Devil's advocate here?" I blurt.

She leans forward a bit. "I'm trying to get you to see things differently. Not everything is black and white. There are shades of gray too. A lot of times the gray is where we find our answers."

I don't say anything for a few minutes.

"I'm angry at my sister." The words are so quiet they're barely audible, but she hears them anyway.

"That's normal."

"I hate being angry at her. I loved her more than anyone. But ... but apparently she didn't love me enough to stay."

Dr. Lee appraises me for a minute. "When people take their lives, it's not because they don't care about their loved ones, it's because they don't love *themselves* enough. They're haunted by their own thoughts and death becomes the only peace they can seek, the only control they have."

"I don't want to stay angry at her," I admit.

"Of course you don't."

"How do I move past it?" My lower lip trembles.

"I'm not here to give you answers. There are no true answers to these kinds of questions, but my advice is to give yourself a chance to *feel* the anger. If you've been blocking it, or feeling guilt for it, you're not allowing yourself the proper chance to grieve. It's okay to be angry, or sad, or happy, or whatever you need to feel in the moment. Whether it's to do with your sister or not. We're all entitled to our emotions."

I wipe at my tears. I don't know when they started. That seems to be happening a lot lately.

"I don't know how I'm going to live the rest of my life without her."

That, right there, has been the thing plaguing me the most.

There are so many things we'll never get to share. Fourteen years is too little time with her. It scares me knowing that one day I'll have to deal with the fact that she's been dead longer than she was alive, and that is terrifying.

"You know," I begin, my breath stuttering, "maybe it would've been easier if she'd died in a car accident or something. She wouldn't have chosen to leave then."

Dr. Lee frowns. "It still would hurt. You'd still be

angry. The emotions would just be directed elsewhere. To the other driver if one was involved, the weather if that was the culprit, it's always easiest to find a fall guy than to just deal with things as they are."

I nod, plucking a tissue from the side table. She's right, I know it.

I've been finding excuses for everything for far too long and burying the emotions I didn't want to feel or deal with down deep.

"You coming here is a big step in the right direction, Violet. It may not seem like it, but it is."

I nod, looking at the time.

My hour is up already.

"Come back," she almost pleads with me. "You don't have to shoulder every burden on your own."

I push up from the chair and look back at her. "Thank you."

As I walk out, I feel a little lighter, like I'm finally heading in the right direction. I have a long way to go, but suddenly life doesn't feel so daunting.

CHAPTER THIRTY-THREE

The pile of letters from various colleges stare up at me.

"Are you ever going to open them, Vi?" My dad's voice sounds behind me and I jump back from the kitchen counter like I've been electrocuted.

I've been letting the letters gather here for several weeks now and haven't opened a single one, but today they taunt me, because my wild card school finally sent one.

I lied when I told Lydia I was undecided on what I wanted to do with my life, but the fact remains this is a recent development and me entirely going out on a limb.

The big black NYU letters shine back at me from the thick envelope.

"I guess I should start." My eyes flick from him to the stack.

He peeks over my shoulder. "NYU, huh? Didn't know you applied there."

"It was just for fun," I murmur, lying easily.

I might have gotten coerced into the theatre production of Beauty and the Beast, but I found a passion there I wasn't expecting.

I love transforming into a character, living their life, and giving them a voice, a vessel to exist.

So, I applied to NYU for acting.

I don't think I'll be accepted, and I know that'll disappoint me even though it shouldn't. Acting isn't something I ever planned on, it just sort of happened, and I should strive for something practical. Useful. But I also want to be happy, and doesn't that mean choosing something I love?

I pick up one of the envelopes and open it.

We regret to inform you…

I open another.

Acceptances and rejections pile up until there's only one left, the only one that matters to me.

I pick up the envelope from NYU, looking at my dad as my mom enters the room.

It feels like my entire life hangs on the answer waiting for me on this simple slip of paper.

"Oh, you're opening them," my mom says joyously, hurrying over to us. "Only one left? Why didn't you tell me you were opening them?"

"Sorry, I just decided to go for it." I bite my lip and look between them. "Dad?" He peaks a brow at my tone. "I … I lied when I said I applied just for fun. I…" I swallow thickly. "I've really loved everything to do with being in the play, and I've found something I'm passionate about so ... I decided to apply to NYU ... for acting."

They both stare at me in surprise. "Vi, that's awesome." My mom claps her hands.

"R-Really?" I stutter. "I thought you might be mad."

My dad reaches out and pulls me into a hug. "We want you to be happy. That's what we've always wanted."

I hug him back and dammit if I'm not going to cry. "I love you guys."

My mom joins the hug and the three of us stand there holding each other.

After a moment we break apart and they look at me expectantly.

"Open it," my mom encourages, her smile wide.

"Do it." My dad nods at the unopened letter.

I break it open and shake my head as I exhale a breath.

I slip the papers out.

A smile splits my face.

"I've been accepted."

My dad picks me up and spins me around and I laugh hysterically, because the sign I didn't know I was looking for is here.

CHAPTER THIRTY-FOUR

The weeks pass in a blur and before I know it, it's April Fool's Day.

Or better known around these parts as opening night.

Mr. Rochester runs around backstage barking orders and sweating so much his shirt is soaked.

I put on Belle's opening outfit and Lydia bustles around me, smoothing it in places and making sure everything is perfect with it. My hair is braided and tied with a blue string. I don't have much makeup on, just a little mascara and blush for my cheeks.

I can hear the soft rumble of voices as people pile into the theater. My parents are out there somewhere. I'm sure Finn's mom is there too, and I know from Lydia that Husten has come in. I'm not sure if Della came too.

"Are you nervous?" Lydia asks me, clipping a loose thread.

I nod, running my fingers down the fabric as I look in the mirror. "Yeah, I think I'd be crazy not to be. But I'm excited."

"You're going to kill it," she assures me, taking a few steps back and looking everything over.

"Five minutes!" Mr. Rochester calls out from somewhere. His voice is so loud I wouldn't be surprised if the whole auditorium heard him.

"How he hasn't suffered a heart attack is beyond me," Lydia murmurs with a soft laugh.

"He looks close to a stroke," I note as he runs by, dripping in sweat with a headset on and his trusty clipboard held tightly in his hand.

"I'm stealing that clipboard from him. Mark my words," Lydia warns. "When it vanishes, don't tell on me."

I laugh. "Do you have a death wish?"

"No, I just really hate that clipboard."

"Two minutes!"

"I better get in place," I tell her.

She gives me a thumbs up. "You've got this, Violet."

I squeeze her hand in thanks and head towards the stage.

"Nebula?"

I turn around to find Finn is his Beast makeup and clothes.

"Yeah?" I pause, tilting my head to the side.

He clears his throat. "Break a leg."

I give him a small smile. "You too."

I've seen Dr. Lee a few more times, and my anger has lessened. I don't find myself getting mad every time I look at Finn. I still don't understand what happened to us, but I'm letting it go. Dr. Lee has taught me I can't control everything.

"Show time, everyone!"

And with Mr. Rochester's final yell, the curtains go up, and it begins.

———

"You were brilliant, sweetie." My mom presses a kiss my cheek, pride radiating off of her.

"Thank you." I smile back at her, glowing from the inside out.

"We're so proud of you." My dad pulls me into a hug, the flowers he brought for me getting squished between us. "Oh, uh, these are for you." He pulls away and hands me the bouquet. It's a mix of different flowers, and I take them from him, smelling one of the large lilies.

I was worried something might go wrong, but the entire play went off without a hitch. This felt like a monumental moment in my life, the start of something big. I'm still surprised by my parents support of me going to NYU. They haven't once told me I'm crazy, and I think after tonight they truly see why I want to do this.

"Hey, Violet, you going to the cast party?" Joe, the guy who played Chip, pauses beside me.

"No." I wave him off. "I'm having dinner with my parents."

"Oh, okay. We'll miss you."

He's barely moved away when my mom gets my attention. "You should go to the party. You don't need to hang out with us."

"I'm not in the partying mood." It's the truth too. "I'd much rather go to dinner with you guys and go home."

"Are you sure?" My dad asks.

"Positive."

After I change my clothes I follow them out to the parking lot.

I spot Finn and his siblings, Della did come, and mom. I lift my hand in a wave and he waves back. There's a look on his face I can't quite decipher. It's perhaps a little sad and maybe longing.

Husten waves at me so I wave back and Della looks over with a smile.

Finn drops his head and I notice Husten say something to him.

I don't see anymore as I climb into the SUV and we drive away.

My parents take me to a fancy restaurant downtown. I've never been before, but assume they have. I don't bother telling them I would've been happy with something simple, because I know they want to make tonight special.

We're seated and I look over the menu.

The cheapest thing on the menu is fifty dollars. They really are going all out. Damn.

After our order is placed they start talking.

"The play. NYU. Graduation soon," my dad rambles. "So many big things are happening."

"Don't forget prom," my mom adds.

I snort. Prom. I don't plan on going. It's in only a few weeks and I don't see the point. Maybe at the beginning of the year I would've wanted to go, but the one person I'd want go with is a stranger now, and he wouldn't attend anyway.

"I'm not going."

She gasps, like a true shocked inhale of breath as if I've personally offended her with this announcement. "Violet, you have to go! It's prom!"

"I don't have to do anything." I take a sip of my fancy water—fancy, because it's in a wine glass.

"It's your senior year," she rambles, her words slurred with desperation. "You'll regret it if you don't."

"Maybe I'll regret it if I do," I argue back in a calm tone, simply trying to get her to see another side.

"Well," she rests her hands on the table, "I think you should give it a little more thought before you decide completely. Maybe we should go look at dresses just in case, since it's so soon. Maybe that girl ... what's her name? Lucy?"

"Lydia," my dad interjects.

"Yes." She snaps her fingers. "Lydia. Maybe she'd like to go?"

She looks so eager, so excited, that I can't say no. "Yeah, that would be okay."

When her smile lights her eyes I know I've made the

right decision. Besides, looking at dresses doesn't mean I'm going to the dance.

Our food is brought out and I push all thoughts of the dance from my mind, instead focusing on this night with my parents. Soon, I won't have times like these with them. I'll be off at college, starting a whole new adventure.

CHAPTER THIRTY-FIVE

"Come on, girls. This way." My mom plows through the shopping mall on a mission.

Lydia and I struggle to keep up with her she moves so easily through the crowd.

Somehow, after I told Lydia about dress shopping I was talked into going as her "date" since she can't go with Husten and, in her words, I can't go with who I want.

"Your mom moves fast." She sounds winded as we pick up our pace.

"When she's on a mission this is how it goes." We reach the department store and lose sight of my mom. "Where's the dress section?" I ask a passing employee and she points me in the right direction.

Lydia and I cross the store in the direction she indicated and find my mom already going through racks of dresses, several already slung over her arm.

Before I can even look at anything I find myself being ushered into a dressing room and having dresses handed to me. The first one I try on is hot pink and fitted, not my kind of dress at all, but I put it on anyway.

Stepping outside I make a face of disgust.

"Nope, not that one," my mom confirms, shoving me back into the dressing room.

I hear her urging Lydia into another room beside me.

I slip on a short white dress with a tulle skirt.

"This doesn't say prom to me," I announce, stepping outside the curtain. "I look like I'm going to get ice cream in a really fancy dress for a fake photo shoot."

My mom laughs. "That was a very dramatic description, Vi. Try another."

I sigh, sulking into the room. Trying on clothes is the bane of my existence. I loathe it. I'd rather do Calculus or Physics and I hate both things with a passion.

After trying on more dresses than I can count, I'm about to call it a bust when my mom announces, "I think this is the one."

Before I can protest she passes another one through the small slit in the curtain.

I take it and everything stops.

My thoughts.

My breath.

My heart.

I stare at the dress with a mixture of awe and longing.

It's loose, but flowy, with sleeves. It's a midnight blue

color with sheer areas, but that's not what takes my breath away.

It's the golden glittery stars and constellations sewn into the fabric that does that.

The stars mean so much to me now. They remind me of Finn, of a friend and love, and how vastly big this world is and we're so small.

A part of me doesn't want to put the dress on, but I can't help myself.

It fits like a glove, as if it was handmade for me.

I smooth my hands down the fabric, taking in the stitched detailing.

I don't have to leave this room to know I'm going home with this dress.

"Come on, Vi. Let me see."

I slide the curtain back and my mom gasps, her hands flying to cover her mouth.

"You're gorgeous, Vi."

"Wow." Lydia's jaw drops as she too exits her dressing room in a beautiful white gown with flowers.

I turn to the mirror in the middle of the changing area and it's even more perfect than I originally thought. It looks like a one of a kind piece.

"You ... you look like a woman," my mom chokes up.

"I feel like one," I murmur.

The person who stares back at me is grown up and glowing. While her eyes are a tad bit sad, there's something else there, a resilience.

No matter what life throws at me, only I have the power to let it knock me down.

Lydia steps up beside me, resting her head on my shoulder. "We look hot."

I laugh. It's genuine, taking over my whole face, my whole being.

"Want to break some hearts with me?" Her eyes sparkle with laughter.

I nod. "Let's do this thing."

CHAPTER THIRTY-SIX

D ESPITE MY INITIAL RELUCTANCE TO GO TO PROM, I end up going all out—well, my mom does. She insists I get my hair, makeup, and nails professionally done. It seems like a waste to me personally, but she wants to do it so here we are.

After hours of feeling like my entire body has been buffed and polished it's time for me to put my dress on. My hair cascades down my shoulder in a loose braid, and when I described my dress to the hair stylist she added shimmery golden thread into it that reflects every time I move. Even my makeup looks like the starry night and my nails are painted a deep blue with a gold glitter polish over top. I slip the dress and heels on and look in the mirror.

The breath is sucked out of my lungs and I can't believe the woman standing in front of me is *me*.

I look like a character from a Shakespearean play or a goddess, maybe Nyx herself.

Even though I didn't want to go, I'm suddenly grateful I am. This isn't a moment I should miss out on.

I grab my matching clutch and stick my phone and some cash inside before I carefully take the stairs down. I haven't worn heels in a long time and I'm out of practice.

My parents meet me in the foyer and my mom promptly bursts into tears.

"Please, don't cry," I beg. "Then I'll cry and I can't ruin my makeup."

"You're right, you're right," she chants, grabbing a tissue off a side table and dotting her eyes.

"You look beautiful, Vi." My dad clears his throat, looking visibly upset.

"So grown up," my mom adds, clutching her chest and holding back more tears.

The doorbell rings and my mom exclaims, "Oh, that must be Lydia!"

She rushes to open the door and Lydia stands on the front porch with her parents.

After a million pictures of the two of us as well as separate ones, we're sent on our way in Lydia's car.

"We're free!" She cries, turning the volume up on her playlist.

"This year has gone by so fast." I look out the window at the passing scenery as she drives to the hotel downtown hosting the prom. "Graduation isn't far away."

"Yeah, it has." She sounds a little sad. "It's like life decided to speed up."

"That's a good way to put it," I agree.

Trying to move on with my life after the pain of losing Luna last year has been tough. Dr. Lee has helped show me I don't need to mask the pain, but embrace it instead, because the loss of my sister isn't something I'm going to forget. Some days will be easier, others harder, but I have to focus on the positive.

And I remind myself that I have to live my life because she didn't get to live hers.

Lydia pulls up to the hotel and they take her car. Heading inside we pass on our tickets, before entering the room.

Both of us pause, in awe of the space in front of us. The theme this year is Paris, and while it sounds cliché to me, this is anything but. There's a mini Eiffel Tower made from what looks like metal, with small lights attached that twinkle. From the ceiling different stars hang, somehow seeming to glow. Tables are dotted around the room with shimmery black fabric and the refreshment stand is against the back wall. Most people seem to be gathered there.

A fast-paced song comes on and Lydia grabs my hand and swings in front of me to tug me forward. "We have to dance!" She pulls me with her, not giving me a chance to protest, and I let myself just go with it.

Live in the moment, I remind myself. *We're not guaranteed tomorrows, and whatever happens, I want to make the most of it.*

One song bleeds into another and after a while I don't know how many we've danced to, but my skin is damp with perspiration and I'm dying of thirst.

"Let's get a drink," I plead.

She looks like she wants to protest, but eventually nods.

I grab two mini water bottles from the table and pass her one. I gulp the whole thing down in seconds and grab another one.

"This is pretty fun." She looks around the room at everyone dancing or occupying a table.

"Come on," this time I grab her hand, "let's dance some more."

"Oh. My. God." Her gaze holds steady on the entrance to the room.

"What? What is it?" I follow her gaze. "Oh, my God," I blurt, jaw dropping in surprise.

I watch Finn stand awkwardly in front of the large double doors, his hands shoved into the pockets of his tuxedo pants. His eyes dart around the room behind his glasses, searching for something. His hair is a little shorter, no longer brushing the top of his glasses, and I bet he got it cut today.

"Go." Lydia bumps me with her shoulder.

"Why?"

She rolls her eyes at me. "He's here for *you*. There's no other reason Finn would brave this, and without Jack at that."

I hadn't even realized Jack wasn't with him.

"H-He's not here for me," I argue. It doesn't seem plausible. There has to be some other reason, an explanation. When I spoke to him about homecoming at the beginning of the school year he was adamantly against it, so coming to prom? It can't be because of me, that would make no sense.

His wandering gaze stops when he spots me.

My breath stops completely as he moves through the crowd. He's careful not to touch anyone and I continue to stand where I am, completely frozen.

"Go." Lydia gives me a small shove. "Stop being dumb and get your man."

I shake my head, but somehow I'm spurred forward.

I keep my eye on Finn's dark bobbing head and we meet in the middle of the dance floor. No one pays us any mind.

"What are you doing here?"

He looks at me steadily, but I notice his shoulders are a little shaky with nerves.

"I saw you leave."

"And you just happened to have a tux?" I accuse.

He wets his lips. "My mom got me one. Just in case I decided to go. So here I am."

"But, why?"

"For you." He taps his fingers against the side of his leg.

My brows furrow. "You're the one that walked away from me, Finn."

"I know." He clears his throat, looking at his shoes. "I ... I thought it was for the best."

"For the best? That makes no sense."

He bites his lip. "That night, having that woman berate me, make me feel less than human while you stood there defending me ... I saw ... I saw a flash of what our future could look like and I didn't want that for you. You shouldn't have to defend me. You deserve someone normal, who you can love without sacrifice."

Tears sting my eyes as I stare at him, at the boy who stole my heart and never gave it back. "Loving you would *never* be a sacrifice."

"I thought you belonged with someone better, someone *more* than I can ever be."

"But ... you're *everything*, Finn."

He reaches out like he wants to touch me but his hand falls back to his side.

"I thought I was giving you a choice by walking away from you—a chance at a normal life. Things will never be easy with someone like me."

I shake my head back and forth. "You think you're so different, but you're not. Everyone has quirks, nobody is *normal* or perfect—but you're the closest thing to it for me. And Finn?" He lifts his head and pushes his glasses up his nose. "I never had a choice when it comes to loving you, I just *do*. That's how love works. You don't choose, you just know."

"And you love me?" Despite him being here, in spite of everything, he still doesn't see how deeply I feel for him. It's like he can't grasp it. Maybe it's because love isn't something you can see. The only proof it exists is in the feeling.

"I do." I nod my head up and down, fighting back tears.

"I love you, too, Nebula."

I remember how he once told me he wasn't sure he knew how to love, if he was even capable of the feeling, but he says it wholeheartedly and I know it's true. I see the love shining in his eyes.

This time he does reach out and he takes my hand. "I'm not sure I'll ever believe I deserve you, but I'm going to try to be worthy."

"You already are."

I move in and kiss him. His other hand cups my cheek, angling my head back as he deepens the kiss. His kiss feels like an apology, but also like a door opening, to another chapter, a new us.

I've always told myself, that whatever happens everything will be all right.

That feels truer now than before. So much has been dealt my way, but I'm dealing with it. I'm growing as a person, learning about myself, letting go of pain.

He breaks the kiss, but keeps a hold on my cheek, resting his forehead against mine.

"Why now? It's been months. We've barely spoken, you rarely look my way, it—"

"Because I couldn't stop thinking about you. Because the hurt never went away. Because despite everything, I want to be the right guy for you. And when I looked at you, I could see the hurt in your eyes, and I knew you must feel this too. I'm not used to this feeling." He brings his other hand over his heart. "Love is an unusual concept to me. I never thought I would experience this kind of love, but you've proved me wrong, and I'm an idiot to throw that away because of fear. No one else's selfish behavior should have any bearing on my decisions, on my *life*."

"I thought I did something horrible to you." I feel the tears coming again, damn them.

"No." He shakes his head. "You did something magical for me. You saw me when no one else did."

"Finn," I breathe, his name the only word my brain can conjure.

He rubs his thumb against my cheek. "You made me feel like I *belonged* when I spent my whole life feeling like an outsider." He wipes a tear off my cheek. "I wasn't looking for you, I didn't ask for you, but you found me anyway. Thank you." He lowers his lips to my ear and I close my eyes. "You saved me, Nebula. You gave me a reason to keep my feet on Earth. I don't have to search the stars for meaning anymore. Not when I have you."

I crash my lips to his, silencing him. My arms wrap around his shoulders, and behind my closed lids the lights flash and twinkle, bright spots in the darkness.

Stars.

Finn might've found a reason to stay planted on Earth, but I found my bright spot in the night sky.

I found *him*.

CHAPTER THIRTY-SEVEN

End of Summer

Time seems to have sped up and there's no slowing it.

In the blink of an eye prom turns into graduation, graduation turns into summer, and summer ... well, it always has to come to an end, right?

My suitcases are packed, and tomorrow my parents drive me to NYU. Lydia is heading there too, studying fashion design, so at least I'll know someone. I'm excited for the opportunities there, to grow and learn. Finn will be heading south to the Georgia Institute of Technology. It's not a surprise to me at all that he'll be pursuing aerospace engineering.

This new chapter of my life is thrilling, but also terrifying. It's my first step into the real world.

It's crazy to think about the fact this time a year ago we were just moving in. So much has happened in that time, but one thing is for certain, I'm in a much better place.

I've continued to see Dr. Lee, and funny enough, I'll miss her while I'm in New York.

Will stirs in his cage, he'll be staying here with my parents since ferrets in dorms aren't exactly allowed. I turn my head and look at the clock on my nightstand.

Three in the morning.

I can't sleep, but not because I'm worried or dwelling on things I shouldn't.

I sit up and pad over to the window, a grin splitting my face when I see my boyfriend, the guy I love, looking up at my window.

He nods his head toward the meadow and I signal back.

Sliding my feet into a pair of slippers I sneak outside. He's waiting for me and reaches for my hand. "For old times sake?"

I slip my hand in his in reply.

I giggle as we run through the tall grass and sink into it, lying on our backs. It's a clear night, no clouds in sight, with a new moon.

That feels significant somehow, like it's reflecting this new beginning in our lives.

Finn and I have fought so hard to get to this moment.

Our childish doubts and insecurities nearly got in our way of a pretty epic love. It's an untraditional love, but it's ours. I wouldn't have it any other way.

His hand is warm and tight around mine. Everything about him feels like it was made for me. I lay my head on his shoulder, curling into his body.

"I'll miss these nights with you."

"I'll miss *you*." His lips brush my forehead.

We're about to head in two very different directions. A lot of couples don't make it past high school, and we had our own major rough patch with him thinking I deserved more than him, but we're past it. Now, I can see where he was coming from, how he thought he was protecting me, saving me in a way, but it was him I needed not anyone else. We don't choose who we love, we just do.

Finn only saw our differences, while I saw our similarities.

But now, we stand on the edge of the world, two who've become one.

"Whatever happens," I murmur against the skin of his neck, "we'll always have the stars."

He kisses me softly, cradling my cheek in his hand. "The stars have burned for a millennia, and we will too."

Just then, a star shoots across the sky.

Finn's words echo in my head from long ago.

"I don't believe wishes come true, but that doesn't mean they aren't worth making."

So, under that night sky, wrapped in the arms of the boy I love, I make a wish.

EPILOGUE

10 YEARS LATER

I LEAN AGAINST THE BALCONY RAILING, A WISTFUL smile touching my lips as I gaze at the night sky.

I didn't used to think much about the night sky, not until I met a boy.

That's how most stories start, I guess. With a boy.

This boy in particular had a major impact on my life, and I can't help thinking about him every time I sit under the stars. He taught me so many things, how important it is to include people, how we're not as different as we think, and how powerful love can truly be even when it's young love.

I remember nights lying in the grass talking with him. Sometimes with only our pinkies touching. Other times enveloped completely in his warm embrace.

Every time I think of him my heart aches a little for

those young people we were. We knew so little about the world, but we felt so much. I guess that sums up being a teenager pretty well.

Arms wrap around me, hands pressing against my swollen and heavily pregnant belly, before a chin rests on my shoulder.

"What are you thinking about?" My husband's deep voice rumbles in my ear and I lean my head against his shoulder, closing my eyes.

"A boy."

He lets out a small chuckle. "A boy, huh? Should I be jealous?"

I turn in his arms, resting my arms around his shoulders. I can't get very close to him, not with my belly in the way.

"No. I think you'd like this boy." I smile up at him, my stomach somersaulting.

Despite all the years we've been together, Finn still makes my body react crazily.

"I hope he treated you well." He brushes his nose against my cheek.

"The best," I exhale, meeting blue eyes behind a pair of glasses. "I love you." I brush my lips against his.

Despite the odds, with everything stacked against us, we've made it.

Maybe it's crazy to marry your first love, but I think I knew from the start Finn was meant to be all my firsts and my lasts. He might not have believed it, but I did, deep down I always knew he was it for me.

"I love you, Nebula, more than you'll ever know, and

little Moon too." He touches my belly. "I can't wait to meet our son."

I gasp, feeling a small bit of wetness creep down my leg. I've been having contractions all day, but I thought they were Braxton Hicks.

"I think you're going to meet him tonight."

"What?" His lips part in surprise, blue eyes widening.

"He's coming," I confirm, "we need to go."

Finn goes into action, gathering my things and everything we packed for this moment.

There's no moon in the sky tonight, but soon our Moon will be on Earth with us.

Finn might not have realized his dream of going to outer space, but it's coming to him in our tiny little miracle. It also feels like a bit of Luna is being given back to me. After all, I always called her my Moon.

I don't tell him that night, but some wishes, they do come true.

Check out one of my other Young Adult titles

THE OTHER SIDE OF TOMORROW

Life can change in an instant...

For Willa Hansen, this statement couldn't be truer. One minute she was a seemingly normal fourteen-year-old, and the next her life was turned upside down with only a few words. Three years later, she's receiving a kidney transplant and can start living again, only now she's not sure she knows how.

Life can end in a moment...

Jasper Werth knows this all too well, seeing as a drunk driver killed his little brother. He's always been a carefree guy, never taking life too seriously, but losing his brother is a major blow, and he finds himself lost until Willa walks into his life.

Life can mend the most broken parts of our souls...

Willa and Jasper couldn't be more opposite, but as fate brings them together they'll learn maybe they're not so different after all.

Sometimes what you need comes in a package you least expect.

ACKNOWLEDGMENTS

To my girls Barbara Doyle and Kellen Rhodes, thank you for endless words of encouragement. You keep me from going insane and I'm so thankful for your friendship. Also, Barb, I might joke about being your Momager, but you help and guide me just as much. I'm so glad you're my friend.

Raquel and Stefanie, thank you for two of the best and most patient betas out there. Love you, ladies!

Letitia Hasser, thank you for creating this stunning and unique cover that perfectly captures Finn, Violet, and the theme of stars and space. You brought my vision to life and then some.

Regina Bartley, you're always such a source of encouragement and an amazing friend.

Emily Wittig, you've been in my life for seven years now. You're not only a best friend, but a sister. I miss you, sis, and can't wait until the day I get to squeeze you again! Seriously, prepare for a bone-crushing hug.

Jordan, you're my cousin, family, the sister I always wanted. Without you life would be so dull. Thank you for being you and making me laugh and giving me someone to confide in. Love you, George. ;)

Readers thank you so much for taking a chance on this book. I hope Violet and Finn's book meant as much to you as it has to me.

Lastly, to my brother Noah who served as part of the inspiration behind Finn. You're the sweetest, kindest soul on this planet. I wish more people saw that. But I see you, and you shine the brightest. I don't say it enough, but I love you.